DRAGON LEGEND

READ ALL OF THE BOOKS IN THE
DRAGON REALM
SERIES!

DRAGON MOUNTAIN

DRAGON LEGEND

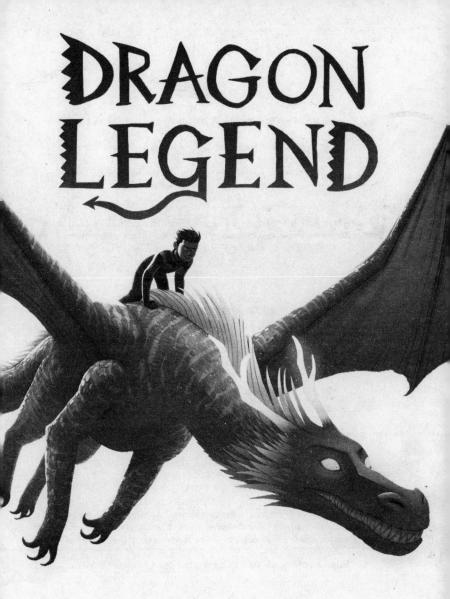

DRAGON LEGEND

KATIE & KEVIN TSANG

SIMON & SCHUSTER

First published in Great Britain in 2021 by Simon & Schuster UK Ltd

3 5 7 9 10 8 6 4 2

Simon & Schuster UK Ltd
1st Floor, 222 Gray's Inn Road
London WC1X 8HB

www.simonandschuster.co.uk
www.simonandschuster.com.au
www.simonandschuster.co.in

Simon & Schuster Australia, Sydney
Simon & Schuster India, New Delhi

A CIP catalogue record for this book is available from the British Library.

PB ISBN 978-1-4711-9309-5
eBook ISBN 978-1-4711-9310-1
eAudio ISBN 978-1-4711-9987-5

This book is a work of fiction. Names, characters, places and incidents are either the product of the author's imagination or are used fictitiously. Any resemblance to actual people living or dead, events or locales is entirely coincidental.

Printed and bound by CPI Group (UK) Ltd, Croydon, CR0 4YY

MIX
Paper from
responsible sources
FSC® C020471

To Rachel and Claire,
for believing in our dragons

Stars

The stars see everything.

And they never forget.

They watch all that happens down below and never interfere. They are constant.

At least most of the time. Because sometimes they shake free from their home in the sky and fly through the dark. Wishes are made on their flaming tails, and when they land they can change history, for better or for worse.

And sometimes, sometimes, stars are pulled down from the sky. But at great cost.

One dragon thought they knew the cost of swallowing a star. And hoped it would be worth it.

A Drop Of Blood

Deep inside Dragon Mountain, Billy Chan held a blade made of bone.

He stood at the edge of a shimmering blue pool. Next to him were his friends Charlotte Bell and Liu Ling-Fei. JJ was there too, but he wasn't a friend. Not yet – maybe not ever.

And behind them were dragons.

In what felt like a lifetime ago, but in reality was just a matter of days, Billy and his friends had opened the mountain, discovered four dragons with hearts that matched their own and linked with them for ever in a rare and ancient bond.

Now, the dragons and their humans gazed into the

shimmering pool. Spark – a blue-and-gold dragon with a long neck, twisting gold antlers and giant sheer wings – stared the most intently. Her gold eyes crackled with focus. Billy sensed her effort through their bond and tried to send her strength.

'Are you sure this is going to work?' said Charlotte, frowning. 'Didn't it take Dimitrius and the nox-wings almost one hundred years to make a portal? Can we really have made one in just a few days?'

'It has to work,' said Billy brusquely. He couldn't bear to think about the alternative.

It had been two days since their friend Dylan O'Donnell had been taken by Old Gold, who ran the summer camp at the base of Dragon Mountain where they had all been campers. Old Gold, whom they had trusted as a mentor. Old Gold, whom Ling-Fei had viewed as a surrogate grandparent, but who had in fact murdered her real grandparents. Old Gold, who had a heart as evil as the Dragon of Death's own and was getting steadily closer to finding her.

If that happened, the Dragon of Death would be stronger than ever. Her hunger for power was endless, and all would suffer for it.

The guilt of losing Dylan hung heavy on Billy. He felt as if he should have been able to save his friend. He hadn't smiled since Dylan had disappeared into the nox-wing portal.

'It *will* work,' said Ling-Fei. Even after everything that had happened, her optimism wasn't dampened. Billy knew Old Gold's betrayal had hurt her deeply, but Ling-Fei chose to focus on finding Dylan. That was something Billy admired about Ling-Fei: her ability to see the best in people no matter what.

'Buttons should go first,' said Tank, Charlotte's huge red dragon, who barely fitted inside the underground grotto in which they were crammed. 'With the other child.'

'My *name* is JJ,' muttered JJ.

'Must I travel with him?' said Buttons plaintively. Buttons – a green dragon with a long snout, thick tail and protruding belly – had bonded with Dylan. Everyone was counting on the strength of their tie to pull Buttons to whatever time and place Dylan and Old Gold had jumped to. There, they would also find the Dragon of Death – and, if everything went to plan, they would stop her once and for all.

'Yes,' said Xing, Ling-Fei's slender silver dragon. 'His connection to his grandfather will help make sure that we travel to the right time.' Her sharp golden eyes softened. 'I do not doubt your bond with Dylan, but we must take every precaution. You know this.'

Buttons sighed and looked at JJ. 'I hope you don't fall off,' he said. 'Without the human-dragon heart bond, riding dragons is much more difficult. You will have to stay focused and hold on tight.'

Billy put a hand on Spark and felt grateful for their bond that enabled him to fly through the sky with Spark as if he were part of her. Their connection was so deep that they could even share each other's thoughts when they were close.

A few days ago, Billy would have found the idea of getting on a dragon completely terrifying, so he could understand why JJ might hesitate. At least Buttons wasn't the scariest of the dragons. Sure, his claws were long and his teeth were sharp, but he didn't snarl like Xing or look as if he could swallow you in one gulp like Tank.

And, if it had been a few days ago, Billy would

have expected JJ to make some sort of sarcastic retort, the kind JJ tossed around back at camp, but now he nodded meekly. He had dark circles under his eyes, and Billy saw that his nails looked bitten and ragged. JJ tugged on the orange bodysuit the dragons had fashioned for him. 'You're sure this thing will protect me?'

'Better than your human clothes,' said Xing. 'Be grateful we were able to provide one.'

Billy, Charlotte and Ling-Fei all wore similar suits, given to them by the dragons when they first knew they were going into the Dragon Realm. The suits were crafted by dragon magic and made of a rare fabric that could withstand the extreme conditions of the Dragon Realm and the harsh blows of battle. The suits had already proven to be the difference between life and death, protecting them from giant crab attacks and deadly blows from enemy nox-wings.

And they had something better than the suits.

They had *pearls*.

Throughout the Human and Dragon Realms there existed eight magical pearls – the Eight Great

Treasures – and with them came powers, some of which were known and some yet to be discovered. Between them, Billy and his friends had four. At least ... Billy *hoped* Dylan still had his pearl.

When they had received their pearls and bonded with their dragons, powers within them had been activated. Superpowers that previously Billy had thought only existed in comic books and movies. Powers that they had needed to survive in the dangerous Dragon Realm. Dylan had the Granite Pearl and the power to charm others into doing what he wanted. Ling-Fei had the Jade Pearl, giving her an affinity for nature and the ability to sense life and magic energy around her. Charlotte had the Gold Pearl, which activated a super-strength within her. And Billy had the Lightning Pearl, boosting his innate physical agility. With the pearl, he was extraordinarily fast and nimble, able to flip and jump with ease. Their combined powers had helped them fight the evil nox-wings, followers of the Dragon of Death who were intent on bringing her back to full strength. But Billy and his friends hadn't anticipated Old Gold's betrayal, which led to Dylan's kidnap when he was pulled by Old Gold into the portal to find the Dragon of Death, leaving behind Old Gold's grandson, JJ.

JJ didn't have a pearl, and over the past two days Billy had sometimes caught JJ gazing at his when he'd untucked his necklace from under his blue-and-gold suit. Even if you didn't have a dragon bond, a pearl on its own would be something worth having. The pearls were so valuable and so powerful that Old Gold had killed Ling-Fei's grandparents for one, even without knowing its true capabilities. Not even the dragons knew everything the pearls could do. Billy was grateful to have the Lightning Pearl and Spark, because he was certain the quest to save Dylan and stop the Dragon of Death was going to be almost impossible. But, with his pearl power, his dragon and his friends, Billy felt as if he might just be able to achieve the impossible.

'Are you ready?' said Tank, drawing Billy back to the present.

The present that was soon to become the past.

Or maybe it was more that the past was soon to become their present. Every time Billy tried to get his head round jumping through time and space, his thoughts jumbled and he felt a bit nauseous.

'I'm ready, but I'm nervous,' admitted Ling-Fei. 'What if it doesn't work? What if something goes wrong?'

'There is always a chance of something going wrong,' said Buttons gently.

'The risks of going far outweigh the risks of not going,' added Tank gruffly.

'I'm doing this no matter what,' said Billy. He looked at his friends, at JJ, at the dragons. 'We have to fix this. We have to stop the Dragon of Death. We have to stop Old Gold.' He resisted glaring at JJ here, because, as much as he wanted to blame him for Old Gold's evil actions, he knew it wasn't fair. 'And we have to save Dylan.'

'I'm with you,' said Charlotte.

'Me too,' said Ling-Fei. 'I know it will be dangerous, but this is what we have to do.'

'JJ?' Billy asked, looking him in the eye. He knew they had a better chance of finding Dylan and Old Gold with JJ, but he didn't want to force JJ to come with them.

'Do I have a choice?'

'You always have a choice,' said Spark, her eyes still focused and glowing as she prepared the portal.

JJ was silent as he weighed his options. 'I'll come,' he said finally. 'I want to find my *yeye*,' which was the Mandarin word for 'grandpa'. He paused and looked down a little nervously. 'And I want to help find Dylan too.'

Billy wasn't sure if they could trust JJ, but he really wanted to. They had enough to deal with without worrying about him too.

'Enough discussion,' said Xing, twining round Ling-Fei. 'We should be on our way.'

'If the humans are ready for their contribution,' said Spark, still not taking her eyes off the shimmering pool. The pool that contained her hoard.

'And if you are ready for this sacrifice,' Buttons said, nodding at Spark. 'It is no small thing for a dragon to give up their hoard.'

'It is for the greater good,' said Spark. She spoke evenly, but Billy felt her tension.

A dragon's hoard was their most precious possession. It was an extension of their essence. Dragons spent years, lifetimes, building up their hoards. And Spark was about to destroy hers by turning it into a portal.

It had to be Spark's. Billy had been shocked when he'd heard what Spark had to do, but she had gently explained that it had to be her hoard because of its precious contents. It contained living plants and fish, as well as stardust, which dragons believed all things were made of, making it more powerful than any of the other dragons' hoards, as precious as they were to them. To create a portal strong enough to break the laws of nature and to travel through time required energy, magic and sacrifice. And all the care and energy Spark had put into her hoard, and all the living energy within it, could be transferred to create the portal. It was a strange magic, she'd said, not quite looking Billy in the eye.

In the sparkling, glowing pool, starfish sat next to swirls of starlight. Tiny seahorses bobbed amid vibrant coral, and rainbow-coloured fish darted through a miniature seaweed forest. When Billy had first seen Spark's hoard, he had added one of his most prized possessions – his lucky shell from a beach in California, from *home*.

But the sacrifice of the hoard on its own, and all the life in it, was still not enough. The portal needed more.

Spark had swallowed a star once to save Billy, and she had done it again to create the swirling portal in front of them. But there was one more thing the portal needed before they could travel through it: the willing blood of all who wished to pass.

The dragons had already made their offerings, their golden blood dripping thickly from their lips. Their teeth were sharp enough to cut even their own steel skin.

That left the humans. The dragons couldn't bite or claw them to get their blood offerings. They had to be given willingly.

So the group had gone back to the place where they had found a mountain of dragon bones. And, while the dragons waited under the three moons that hung in the night sky of the Dragon Realm, Billy, Ling-Fei, Charlotte and JJ had rummaged as respectfully as they could through the bones of dead dragons until they had each found one they could sharpen to a point.

As Billy held his own blade of bone, he hoped none of the others had thought what he had while sifting through the dragon bones. That these were dragons killed in the name of dark magic. And that using living things as fuel for the portal felt a lot like what the Dragon of Death and her nox-wings did.

He hadn't wanted to say it out loud though, because what if the others agreed and they decided not to go through with it and Dylan was left lost in time with the Dragon of Death? And what if the Dragon of Death was then able to return to her full power, and enslave the human world and destroy everything Billy cared about? Demolish the whole world? So what they were doing couldn't be bad. Because Billy knew that they were on the side of good. They were trying to save everyone and everything. Not just Dylan.

'If you're ready,' said Spark, nudging Billy gently on the cheek. Billy knew she was giving more than any of them, using her own power and sacrificing her hoard, and he hoped she knew how much it meant.

Thank you, he told her through their bond.

At first, he thought Spark hadn't heard him, she was so focused on the portal pool, which was swirling faster and faster. Then he felt a rush of warmth.

Of course, she replied. *I can do it. We can do it. Don't be scared.*

And, as the thought hit him, he realized he *had* been scared. Scared of jumping into the unknown. But having his dragon – and his friends – with him gave him a sense of comfort. Spark was right. They could do this.

'I'm ready,' said Billy. He looked at the others, each standing with their own blade of bone at the edge of the swirling pool.

He took a deep breath and pressed his blade against his palm. Blood welled up faster than he thought it would, and, in a moment, a few drops had fallen into the pool. As they did, the water sparked as if hit by an electric current.

Charlotte didn't even blink as she pricked her finger. She glared at JJ. 'Don't wuss out,' she said.

JJ nodded and offered his own drop of blood.

Ling-Fei went last, not looking as the blood dripped out. 'Is it done?' she said.

'It's done,' said Xing, wrapping herself protectively round Ling-Fei. 'And now we go.'

It felt strange, seeing JJ clamber awkwardly onto Buttons. Buttons looked at the others, his expression unusually serious. 'We will see you in a moment,' he said before they disappeared into the portal, JJ's arms clamped tightly round Buttons's thick neck.

The last bit Billy saw of them was the tip of Buttons's thick tail.

Tank looked far too large to fit in the portal, but magic was magic and the portal, very clearly a portal and not a hoard now, expanded imperceptibly to let Tank through.

'Catch you on the other side,' said Charlotte from her perch on Tank's head. 'Let's go, Tank!' And, with a yelp, they tumbled in.

'Come quickly after us,' said Xing to Spark. 'Do not tarry. We might be playing with time, but we don't have much of it.'

'We will. Fly light, fly fast,' said Spark.

'See you soon, Billy,' said Ling-Fei with a smile. 'Don't worry.'

'I'm not worried,' said Billy, even though he could

feel fear cooling his blood. *What if Spark is wrong? What if we end up in the wrong place? And what if I explode in the portal?*

He didn't know if Xing and Ling-Fei heard him as they slipped into the portal, making barely a ripple in the swirling . . . Billy wasn't sure what to call it. It wasn't water any more. It was a whirling silver-and-blue electric current, and it was buzzing and oh, he hoped it wasn't going to hurt.

'Be brave, Billy,' said Spark. She paused. 'I will need your bravery, perhaps most of all.' Before Billy could ask her what she meant, Spark dived in, wings back as if she were jumping from a great height.

As Billy hit the whirling, crackling current, he noticed, absently, that its colour was changing from blue to purple.

Everything surrounding him flashed bright white, like lightning striking all around. More than that, he felt as if he were inside a lightning bolt . . . no, as if he *were* the lightning bolt. He felt a charge run from the tips of his hair all the way to his toes, and he could barely hold onto Spark, but he knew he had to, he *had* to. If he just held onto Spark, everything would be okay. Somehow, in the midst of everything, she must have heard his thoughts because, with a surge, he heard her.

Hold on, Billy.

He wasn't sure if she meant keep holding onto her or 'hold on' as in 'just wait a second' or 'hold on, you've got this', but he decided it meant it all and he held on. Even when the flashing stopped and darkness became so absolute it pressed down on him the way waves crashed on the shore, and he couldn't see, couldn't hear, couldn't feel, couldn't sense *anything*, he held on.

Hope And The Heart Bond

Just when Billy thought he couldn't handle a single second more of the overwhelming and complete darkness, and he was certain he was dying, or maybe already dead, he and Spark tumbled into the light.

Spark landed on her feet but swayed back and forth, clearly disoriented.

Billy scrambled off her back and collapsed to his hands and knees. His lungs hurt and his head felt as if it had been squeezed through a garden hose. He gulped in air and gripped fistfuls of dirt on the ground, needing them as an anchor that he was *somewhere*, even if he didn't know *where* or *when*.

When the ringing in his ears stopped, he heard Charlotte's voice. It sounded as if she were speaking from very far away. 'That was *awful*,' she said. Billy looked up, his vision still cloudy, and saw that she was standing surprisingly close to him, her hand on Tank's foot for balance. Another voice barrelled into his awareness.

'Oh, no, oh, no, oh, no!'

Billy looked in the direction of this new voice. It was Buttons, and he looked as distraught as he sounded.

'What is it?' said Ling-Fei, who was still on Xing's back. Her braids were messy, and she looked faint.

'Is JJ with any of you?' said Buttons.

'Isn't he with you?' demanded Tank.

'I think it is resoundingly obvious that he is not,' said Xing.

Charlotte whipped her head round, her eyes huge. 'Oh, son of a biscuit eater. He really isn't here, is he?'

'What are we going to do?' said Billy, panic rising. He didn't like JJ much but that didn't mean he wanted him to be stuck in a time-travel portal for ever. And, selfishly, he knew if JJ was with them, they had a better chance of finding Old Gold. Which meant a better chance of finding Dylan.

Now that Billy was looking around, trying to see if they'd somehow missed JJ, he was able to take in where they were. And where they weren't. 'Shouldn't we be inside the mountain? Just in a different time?'

'It appears we have moved through both space and time,' said Xing, gazing out at the landscape.

It looked similar to the Dragon Realm that Billy knew, but there were slight differences. A brilliant oval-shaped sun still hung low in the sky, across from three moons that were always visible, but the landscape was unfamiliar.

Instead of bare land and huge, jagged mountains puncturing the sky, they were surrounded by miles and miles of grass that reached up to their knees. The land was so flat that Billy could see all the way to where the sky met the ground. It was beautiful. Billy marvelled at trees covered in gigantic flowers, and floating islands that bobbed up and down in a blazingly blue sky, like buoys out at sea. Strange-looking insects buzzed around them, dipping into the flowers above and the grass below. But, as beautiful as the landscape was, it didn't change the awful situation they were in.

'Buttons, what happened when you were in the portal?' said Ling-Fei gently.

'JJ was with me for ... most of it,' said Buttons, looking shamefaced. Or as shamefaced as it was possible for a dragon to look. 'When he slipped off my back, I tried to grab him, but, oh, you know what being in that thing was like!'

'We all held onto *our* humans,' Xing pointed out.

'He isn't *my* human!'

'You still should not have lost him,' Xing snapped back.

'It wasn't on purpose!' Buttons sounded miserable.

'Stop fighting!' yelled Billy, surprising himself. 'This isn't helping anyone. We have to think.' He stared up at the space above them, where the portal still shimmered strangely.

'We cannot wait for ever for the boy,' said Tank gruffly. 'Time is not on our side. Spark, is he still in the portal? Try to find him.'

Spark, who had been strangely silent since they had arrived, stretched to her full length, her neck long and her wings out. Billy helped Spark focus through their bond, as she tried hard to locate JJ. It was another advantage of their connection: Billy could use it to help Spark magnify her powers.

Her gold eyes lit up. 'Something is coming,' she said. 'It might be him.'

'It'd better be him,' said Charlotte, eyeing the swirling air suspiciously. 'I don't want something or someone else coming through!'

And then with a yelp JJ flew out of the portal and landed face down in the grass. The portal still swirled above him.

Billy went to his side. 'Are you all right?' he said, helping him up.

JJ scowled at him. 'Did you mean for me to get lost in there?'

'What? No! Of course not. How would I even do that?'

'Your dragon set it up, didn't she? All I know is that one second I was with the green dragon and the next I felt as if I was being pulled limb from limb and my eyeballs were going to be sucked out of their sockets. And I was alone.' JJ glared at Buttons.

'It is an untested process,' said Xing smoothly. 'Be glad you arrived at all, and in one piece.'

'I hope we don't ever have to do it again,' said Billy, rubbing his eyes.

'Well, obviously we're going to have to do it again after we find Dylan and defeat the Dragon of Death. We're going home after that, remember?' said Charlotte with the kind of confidence that Billy found both admirable and exhausting.

JJ frowned. 'But where *is* Dylan? And my *yeye*? Wasn't that thing supposed to take us to them? I don't see . . . anyone anywhere.'

Billy found himself grateful that JJ was voicing his own anxieties.

'It appears we are in the far reaches of the Dragon Realm,' said Tank. 'Even if much changed over time, I recognize the mountains that have remained constant through the years.'

'I will see if anything else looks familiar,' said Xing, who had the best vision of all the dragons. She flew high into the sky, until she was barely a speck, before shooting back down. 'I think we have landed near the Forgotten Sea,' she said. 'We are far from any other landmarks I know.'

'So none of us know where we are and the people

we are looking for aren't here,' muttered JJ. Again, Billy had the strange sensation that JJ knew what was worrying him, and, more than that, felt the same way.

'This *is* the time Dylan is in. I'm sure of it,' said Buttons, finally sitting up. 'He's closer. Not close, but closer. Our bond does not feel like a spiderweb as it has these past few days. It feels like something more substantial.'

'I hope Dylan can feel it too,' said Billy. 'I hope he knows we're coming for him.' He looked up at Buttons. 'So, which way?'

Buttons took a breath. 'All I know is that he is near.'

'That isn't enough!' said Billy, fists clenched as his frustration finally bubbled over. 'He could be *anywhere*.' He thrust his arms out. 'And none of you even know this part of the realm!'

Charlotte's eyes narrowed. 'Listen up, Mr Cranky Pants,' she snapped. 'You aren't the only one who misses Dylan or the only one who wants to stop the Dragon of Death. I get that you are sad. But we are *all* sad. We don't have time to be sad right now though. We have to focus. Being sad takes energy, and we need all our energy to SAVE OUR

FRIEND AND THE WORLD!' She ended her speech in a shout with her hands on her hips, breathing heavily.

Billy looked away, embarrassed to be called out in front of the dragons. He knew Charlotte was right.

'Billy, we all want the same thing,' said Ling-Fei quietly.

'I thought we would have a better plan,' said Billy, his words coming as fast as his thoughts. He looked at the dragons' solemn faces. 'We trusted you . . . and now Dylan is missing.'

'We warned you that there would be danger,' said Spark softly.

'But we should have won!' shouted Billy. He felt as if he might cry. 'We were stronger! And we closed the nox-wing portal! We did what we needed to do. If it wasn't for Old Gold, the world would be saved. We'd still have met all of you. Everything would be perfect, and now . . .' He took a shuddering breath. 'We were so close,' he choked out.

JJ cleared his throat. 'Um. I'm really sorry again about what my *yeye* did.' He lowered his gaze and locked eyes with Ling-Fei. 'Both taking Dylan and ... killing your grandparents. I never saw that side of him. The person you knew, the person he was at camp, that was him too. It wasn't all an act. I think he's just become ... I don't know ... power hungry. I hope he can come back to who he is. Who I know he is.'

'Well, I don't care if the Dragon of Death eats him,' said Charlotte, wrapping an arm round Ling-Fei.

'That is unlikely, as this Old Gold is hoping he has a heart to match the Dragon of Death's,' said Tank. 'Although the Dragon of Death has always been unpredictable.'

'And who knows what she would do with a human child in her clutches?' said Buttons. Fear shimmered in his golden eyes.

'Which is why we need to start moving,' said Billy, swallowing his fear and trying to make his voice strong.

'Billy,' Spark said suddenly, turning her gaze on him. 'Buttons and Dylan share a heart bond, but you and the others, your friendship should also help. And –' her eyes lasered in on him – 'that backpack. It's Dylan's, isn't it?'

Billy had almost forgotten about the backpack he was wearing. The one Dylan had carried every day at camp and in the Dragon Realm.

'An item of his *is* helpful,' said Xing, moving forward to inspect it. 'Something closer to him would be better, but this will do.'

'Are you like . . . bloodhounds?' said JJ, scratching his head.

'As offensive as the comparison is,' hissed Xing, 'you aren't completely wrong.'

'And you will all help guide us too,' said Spark. 'Close your eyes and spin slowly. Focus on Dylan. Think of him. Reach out to him. Stop when you feel closest to him.'

'This is ridiculous,' said JJ. 'You want us to spin round with our eyes closed and then we'll magically know which direction to go in?'

'Do you have any better ideas?' Billy said.

'Fine, fine,' said JJ, holding his hands up. 'I'll spin in a circle. As long as I don't need to go into that portal again any time soon.'

'While you focus on Dylan, we'll enchant and hide the portal,' said Spark. She looked at JJ. 'You should focus on your grandfather since he is the one you are closest to.'

Billy closed his eyes and thought about Dylan. He thought about the jokes he made and the stories he told, how he did things even when they scared him. He thought about how much Dylan loved the pork buns back at camp, and the peaches that grew in the Dragon Realm. He thought about Dylan's Irish accent and his love for his sisters in Galway and how he had taught himself Chinese just because he liked languages. Billy thought about how he'd never had a friend like Dylan before – a friend he felt as if he could truly be himself with. And he thought about how, even though there were still four of them with JJ, it felt as if a piece of the puzzle that made things just work was missing. As if he and Charlotte and Ling-Fei were off balance without Dylan.

Billy thought all these things as he slowly spun in a circle, and then he stopped. His eyes fluttered open.

Charlotte, Ling-Fei and JJ had stopped too. Their feet all pointed in the same direction.

'I feel it too,' Buttons rumbled. 'North. I feel a pull to the north.'

'Then north we go,' said Tank. 'Children, take heed, this is a land before our time but not before the time of dragons. The dragons here may not look kindly on humans in their midst.'

'And there are other creatures too,' said Spark. 'Creatures we only know from legend. Creatures we would be wise to avoid.'

Billy shook his head. 'I don't want to know what mythical beasts frighten dragons,' he said. Though, in that moment, he didn't feel frightened. He felt excited. As if they were finally getting somewhere. He rolled his shoulders back and looked at Charlotte, Ling-Fei and JJ. 'I'm ready if you guys are.'

'I'm always ready,' said Charlotte, swinging herself onto Tank's head and settling behind his ears. Ling-Fei leaped onto Xing's back, and Billy clambered into his preferred spot between Spark's wings.

JJ eyed Buttons hesitantly. 'I won't fall off this time, right?' he said.

'I'll do my best to keep you safe,' said Buttons. 'In the air and on the ground. You aren't Dylan, aren't *my* human, but you are a human child. And I pledged long ago to look after humans when I could.'

'I'm thirteen,' said JJ. 'Not a kid like these guys.'

'Yeah, because that one year makes such a difference,' said Charlotte, rolling her eyes.

'Enough,' said Xing. 'Billy is right. We don't have time to waste. And, if you have all sensed something in the north, we should take advantage of that. We don't know how long they will stay in that direction.'

'Let us fly,' said Spark.

The four dragons and four humans took off into the sky, hope and their heart bonds their only guide.

The Forgotten Sea

As a new world unfolded below them, Billy forgot how much was at stake for a moment. The view was like nothing he'd ever seen. He was overwhelmed with wonder.

It looked kind of like he had always imagined the world to be when dinosaurs roamed, and he couldn't shake the feeling that a T-Rex might emerge in the distance. He wondered briefly who would win in a battle between a dinosaur and a dragon. Dragon, definitely.

They flew on and on, low enough to watch for any sign of Old Gold and Dylan. Beneath them, the landscape began to change. The lush and vibrant forests and plains they had flown over shifted to rugged earth and sand.

'Do any of you see the sea?' Spark shouted suddenly.

Billy looked down. He wasn't sure what Spark was talking about, because there was nothing below them, only desert. The others seemed equally confused.

'What do you mean?' said Charlotte.

'I can't see anything!' added Ling-Fei.

'Hold on!' said Spark. She dived downwards, Billy bracing himself because, as always when he flew with her, he could sense what she was going to do as she did it, as if he were an extension of her. She shot further and further down and then said, 'Reach out.'

Billy put his hand out into empty air and gasped. His hand was wet, and then it was in water. As the water connected with his skin, an entire ocean suddenly appeared beneath them.

This must be the Forgotten Sea, he realized.

It stretched on and on. It was a bright tropical blue in parts, turquoise in others, and some patches were so dark they were almost black. Pockets of the sea were so clear that Billy could see far down into the depths. Giant rainbow-coloured fish swam in schools, glistening under the sun.

He laughed as sea spray blew in his face. Next to him, the others dipped their hands in the water, and he heard their shrieks of surprise and delight as the sea appeared around them. It was the happiest Billy had felt since Dylan had been taken.

'I don't understand,' said Ling-Fei, beaming as she ran her hand through the water.

'The Forgotten Sea can only be seen by those who remember it,' said Xing. 'As soon as you touched it, you knew it was there, and it appeared for you. We dragons can see it because of tales we've been told, and now you can see it too.'

Billy took a deep breath, expecting the familiar smell of salt and brine, like the oceans at home. Then he paused. The Forgotten Sea didn't smell of salt. No, the Forgotten Sea smelled like . . .

'Does anyone else smell lemons?' he said, his brow creasing in confusion.

'I can!' said Charlotte. 'I thought my senses were playing tricks on me!'

'It smells like lemons and sunshine,' said Ling-Fei.

She touched her finger to her lips and grinned. 'It tastes like lemons too!'

'At the bottom of the Forgotten Sea are miles and miles of underwater citrus trees,' said Spark with a smile. 'The water is scented with it. Flavoured with it too. And it is safe to drink.'

Billy cupped his palm and drank big gulps of the water. It didn't taste like lemonade, more like icy water that had sliced lemons in it. It was the most refreshing mouthful of water he'd ever had.

'Some of the sea-citrus trees grow tall enough to breach the surface,' said Tank. 'But enough of that – we should keep moving.'

Hours later, when the oval sun was low in the sky and the three moons glowed bright, they turned inland, looking for somewhere to rest for the night.

Billy wanted to keep going, even though he knew they needed a break. He couldn't force the dragons to keep flying through the night, but there hadn't been any sign of Dylan, Old Gold or the Dragon of Death yet, and it made him uneasy. Dylan and Old Gold were already two days ahead of them. Billy told himself that they would make up the distance, because they were flying and Dylan and Old Gold were presumably on foot.

Unless . . .

The thought that Billy didn't want to let himself think wormed its way into his brain.

Unless they had already found the Dragon of Death.

They landed in a clearing near a grove of peach trees. Billy felt strangely comforted by the sight of the trees – at least something was familiar in this time. They had survived on peaches before in the Dragon Realm, and they could do it again.

'This must be a peaceful time for dragons,' said Spark as the others landed nearby. 'Did you see how those dragons were sleeping?' They'd flown over groups of dragons sleeping like lions in a pile, their tails and wings overlapping.

'I did not know dragons could be so . . . familial,' remarked Tank. 'While we have clans and protect one another, usually we sleep independently.'

'Ideally round our hoard,' added Xing.

'I think it's nice,' said Buttons.

'I do too,' said Ling-Fei.

'Y'all, I am not sleeping anywhere dragons could roll over on me,' said Charlotte. Billy silently agreed.

'We are very careful sleepers,' sniffed Xing. 'We would never roll over on someone.' Then her teeth flashed in a sharp grin. 'Unless we meant to.'

Ling-Fei laughed. 'Oh, Xing,' she said affectionately. Billy still marvelled at how Xing, the most cutting and sharpest of all their dragons, was heart-bonded with Ling-Fei, the kindest person he knew. But somehow, despite their apparent differences in temperament, they were a perfect match.

'While the dragons of this time may sleep in the open, it is unwise for us to do so,' said Tank. He looked at Xing. 'Can you sense the Dragon of Death?'

Xing raised her head in the air, her long whiskers twitching. 'Yes. The Dragon of Death is somewhere in this time. I can sense her dark magic. Perhaps those dragons have not come across her yet and do not know that she will make the most of any opportunity to prey on those she deems weaker than herself.'

Billy shuddered. And again hoped that they would

find Dylan and Old Gold before the Dragon of Death did.

'Where are we going to sleep then?' said Charlotte, looking around at the wide, open expanse where they'd landed.

'All of you, come close,' Tank said. When everyone drew near enough to touch one of Tank's mighty wings, he took a deep breath and blew a ring of fire round them. The flames burst towards the sky, leaving them enclosed behind a wall of fire.

'Won't this send a signal to anything flying overhead?' said Billy, pulling at the neck of his suit. He was already starting to sweat. 'You know, like dragons?'

'Patience,' thundered Tank. 'We're not finished.' He looked at Spark and Xing. Together they unleashed a flow of power at the flames. Billy expected it to turn the fire to ice, like Spark had done when Billy and his friends had first encountered the dragons deep in their mountain, but instead it made the flames shimmer and grow higher still, and then they cooled and turned glassy, reflecting what was all around them.

'It is a ring of reflection,' said Buttons. 'Nothing can see in, but we can see out. It is similar to how we enchanted the portal.'

'*That* thing can see in,' said Billy, pointing at a small, round creature buzzing round the top of the ring of reflection.

Xing struck out like a snake, grabbing the small creature in her talons.

There was a squeal.

'Hey!' said Billy, running over. 'It isn't hurting anything!'

'It must have got caught in the enchantment,' said Xing, tossing the creature to the ground. It squealed again and then bounced back up like a ball, its wings buzzing angrily.

The group stared at it. 'Is that ... ?' started Charlotte slowly.

'A flying pig,' Billy confirmed. 'A tiny flying pig.'

The pig was rounder than any pig Billy had ever seen, almost like a balloon with a head and four legs, and had tiny buzzing wings that sprouted from its back.

'I think it's adorable,' announced Ling-Fei.

'Of course you do,' said Charlotte. 'You liked the river creature that took Dylan's pearl too.'

'The river creature that did *what*?' said Tank.

'Never mind,' said Billy quickly. They hadn't told the dragons *everything* that had happened as they had made their way through the Dragon Realm to rescue their dragons from the nox-wings.

'Dylan has his pearl now, doesn't he?' said Buttons, sounding worried.

'He had it when he was taken,' said Billy. 'But I bet Old Gold will try to take it from him.' He hoped that Dylan could keep his Granite Pearl safe from Old Gold. And, even more than that, he hoped Dylan was okay.

'This creature means us no harm,' said Ling-Fei, pointing at the pig with quiet authority. 'I can sense it.'

'I don't know,' said Charlotte warily. 'I still don't trust it.'

The flying pig buzzed over to Charlotte and oinked in her face. Charlotte swatted it away.

Billy laughed despite himself, and the pig oinked again, coming closer to him this time. It had a golden sheen to its skin, making it glow in the night.

'A glow-in-the-dark flying pig,' he said, more to himself than to anyone else. 'Just when I had got used to the idea of dragons, this thing pops up.'

Ling-Fei smiled. 'That sounds like something Dylan would say.'

With a pang, Billy realized she was right. Dylan must have rubbed off on him more than he knew.

'If Ling-Fei says this small, ridiculous-looking creature means us no harm, I believe her,' said Xing. She glared at the other dragons and humans, as if daring them to contradict her. They all knew that Ling-Fei's pearl gave her a supernatural ability to connect with nature.

'How strange that it was caught in the enchantment. That shouldn't happen,' said Spark, studying the small pig as it buzzed closer to Billy. Billy held out a tentative hand, and it landed on his palm. It was no bigger than a baseball but weighed significantly more. He grinned again, unable to feel anything except joy at the sight of the creature.

'It is nothing more than a glorified butterfly,' said Tank with a snort. 'I am weary from flying and do not want to waste any more time discussing this small pest. It can stay if it wants but only if it does not disturb my rest. If it does, I will swallow it whole and that will be that.'

As if it understood, the flying pig shut its eyes, turned in a circle on Billy's hand and curled up, as though it wanted to go to sleep.

'It seems to like you,' said Spark. And then she spoke again – but just to Billy, through their mental connection. *It is good to see you smile, Billy. Smiling now and then will not deter us from our quest.* Her words, along with the joy of the small flying pig, gave Billy a sense of comfort. Spark was right. It felt good to smile. He stroked the little pig between its ears and allowed himself to feel glad that it had stumbled into their group.

'I'm with Tank,' said Charlotte, stretching her arms out as she yawned. 'I'm exhausted.'

'Aren't any of you … hungry?' JJ asked. It was the first thing he'd said since they'd taken flight. Billy noticed he was standing stiffly and realized that dragon flight must have been much more uncomfortable for him because he didn't have a bond with Buttons.

'You're in luck,' said Billy. 'We've got peaches for dinner.'

JJ grimaced. 'Isn't there anything else?'

'They grow everywhere, we know they won't poison us *and* there's the chance that one we eat will make us immortal,' said Billy. He grinned to himself, remembering how much Dylan loved the peaches in the Dragon Realm. 'Obviously we're having peaches again.' The flying pig stirred at the mention of food and its eyes opened. It lifted up into the air, buzzed round the ring and then went up and out of the top of it. Billy hoped it would come back.

'Humans need to eat so frequently,' observed Xing. 'Such a disadvantage to your species. One of many, of course.'

'Don't you also need to eat?' said Billy, frowning.

'Yes, I don't want you to be hungry,' added Ling-Fei, her forehead creasing with worry.

'We can go long stretches of time without eating,' said Spark. 'And, when we do eat, we make sure it is enough to sustain us for a significant amount of time.'

'As long as you don't get hangry,' said Charlotte.

'Hangry?' asked Tank.

'Hungry and angry,' explained Charlotte. 'I would not want to be around a hangry dragon.'

Tank snorted a laugh. 'I suppose I do get a little . . . grumpy if it has been too long since I last ate.'

'We do have an entire sea full of fish nearby,' said Buttons. 'I'm happy to go and catch some. I imagine that peaches, while delicious, might not satisfy everyone's hunger. And we need you all to be at your strongest.'

He rose in the air and flew over the reflective ring.

'He's doing that for you, you know,' said Billy to JJ. 'Even though you aren't his human.' He wanted JJ to be grateful to Buttons, to all of them, for taking him in. But he also felt a begrudging responsibility to reassure JJ that even though he didn't have a dragon bond, they were still all going to watch out for him . . .

'This sucks for me too, you know,' said JJ bitterly. 'Even more than it does for you. My *yeye* is missing. I'm in a world where almost everything wants to eat me. And the one cool thing about it, flying on a dragon, isn't even that great because everyone is always telling me how the dragon isn't my dragon and I'm just temporary. I get it, okay? You all wish Dylan was here instead of me. I'm useful as some sort of tie or whatever to my grandpa, otherwise I'm sure you would have dumped me in that ocean.'

Before Billy could respond, JJ stalked to the other side of the ring that penned them in.

Billy stared after him. He thought about following but realized he didn't have anything to say. It might have been bad for JJ, but, no matter what he said, it was worse for Dylan. And that was whom Billy was worried about.

So he couldn't believe it when Charlotte went up to JJ, put a hand on his shoulder and appeared to be comforting him. Billy turned away, scowling.

'That scowl doesn't suit you,' said Xing, who was curled up nearby. She had one eye open, and Billy realized she must have heard the entire exchange between him and JJ. 'You have a good heart, Billy Chan,' she went on. 'Make sure it stays that way. Hard times shouldn't harden a heart.'

'What does that even mean?' Billy blustered. His ears went hot. Was Xing, the most temperamental of all their dragons, calling him a bad person? 'I just want to find Dylan,' Billy muttered. 'What's wrong with that?'

'You know my meaning, Billy,' said Xing. 'Do not be foolish.' Then her eye closed and she seemed to fall asleep.

Billy sent a rush of frustration down his bond with Spark. *Did you hear that? It isn't fair! I didn't do anything wrong!*

Spark's answer was gentle but firm. *Billy. You know Xing speaks the truth. But you'll feel better in the morning. We all will. Stay focused.* She paused, and then when she spoke again something wavered in her voice. *I need you to stay focused. And I need your heart to guide us. Don't let it harden.*

You could tell if my heart really was starting to change, couldn't you? Billy asked, starting to feel a little bit worried. *You would tell me? Make sure I stayed . . .*

Strong, loyal, brave and true? Billy felt Spark's smile as if he'd seen it. *Yes, I would.* She paused. *Just as I hope you would do with me.*

A Dragon's Dream

Billy had grown used to sleeping on hard ground. The soft grass beneath them tonight felt luxurious compared to the caves they'd slept in before they had jumped through the portal. But still he couldn't sleep.

Xing's words kept ringing through his head. *Hard times shouldn't harden a heart.* Was his heart hardening? Even Ling-Fei had gone up to JJ before they'd gone to bed, and she had more reason than any of them to hate him. Maybe it wasn't fair for Billy to be mad at JJ. After all, JJ didn't want to be here. But Billy couldn't help it.

They'd eaten grilled fish for dinner, the most

filling meal they'd had in days. Buttons had returned with water too, carried in huge leaves cupped like bowls.

The plan was to sleep for just a few hours, and then fly at dawn. Billy turned over onto first one side then the other. He knew he should take advantage of being able to rest. Usually he would have to keep watch for at least a little bit, but the dragons had insisted that they be the ones to keep guard. Charlotte, Ling-Fei and JJ had fallen asleep almost instantly. Billy envied them. Even Spark was curled next to him, wings flat against her back, tail tucked under her. Billy had never seen his dragon asleep.

'Billy,' said a low, gentle voice next to him. His eyes shot open. It was Buttons, a kind expression on his face. 'I can't sleep either. It's why I volunteered for first watch.' He sighed. 'We must stay hopeful. It's the only way.'

A lump formed in Billy's throat. He didn't think he could speak without crying, so he simply nodded. It was all so hard. He was so worried about Dylan. And scared about what it meant that they were in the same time as the Dragon of Death. Could they really defeat her? Billy was trying to stay hopeful, but his thoughts kept going to the worst-case scenarios.

'Would you like me to help you sleep? Like I did in the mountain?'

Billy remembered. Buttons had hummed, the sound like a cello. It was the best lullaby he'd ever heard.

'I'd like that,' he managed now. And he closed his eyes.

But the peaceful lullaby did not follow Billy into his dreams. Instead, he was plagued by terrible nightmares. He dreamed he was in a city on fire. A city full of skyscrapers with roaring dragons wrapped round the spires. There were humans too, all in chains, screaming as the city burned.

He woke with the screams still ringing in his ears.

Above him, the sky was starting to lighten. He sat up and stretched, his heart still pounding. *It was just a dream*, he told himself. *Just a bad dream*. But it had been vivid in a way his dreams had never been before. And it was hard to shake the grip of fear the nightmare had brought.

'It was nice going to sleep and not worrying about

being eaten by some kind of terrifying creature,' Charlotte remarked with a yawn. She'd slept curled up beneath one of Tank's wings.

'I agree,' said Ling-Fei. 'Travelling with our dragons is much better than without them!' She grinned at Charlotte. 'And look, our dragons didn't crush us in their sleep!'

'As I said, we are careful in everything we do.' Xing gently swatted Ling-Fei with the end of her tail and Ling-Fei laughed.

'That was one of the worst sleeps I've ever had,' grumbled JJ. 'What I'd give to be in my own bed again.'

Billy cleared his throat, feeling awkward. He wanted to make things right. He didn't want his heart to harden. 'JJ,' he said, 'I know this is hard for you. I'm glad you're with us though.'

'Really?' said JJ, staring at Billy, unconvinced.

'Yeah,' said Billy. 'Really.'

JJ shrugged. 'Cool,' he said. 'I mean, I still wish I wasn't here, but it is nice to know I'm not completely unwanted.'

Billy looked at the dragons. 'So what's the plan?' he said. 'Do we keep going north?'

'Yes,' said Tank. 'We will continue along the coast unless we sense they have changed direction.'

'Before we go, I need to tell you all something,' said Spark in her whispery voice. Her gold eyes looked tired and Billy noticed a spot in one of them, as if a blood vessel had popped. He felt bad for not noticing how exhausted she was. He should have picked up on it.

'I had a vision last night,' she said. Spark was a seer dragon, but Billy didn't know exactly how her visions worked. How often they came, or whether she had any control over them. He knew she had looked for Dylan and Old Gold, but it had been fuzzy. Maybe she'd finally seen something about them.

As she described the vision, Billy sat bolt upright. She was describing *his* dream. The smoke, the screaming – it matched what he'd seen. Did their connection mean that Billy could somehow share her visions? Before he could blurt out that he had seen the same things, Spark began to describe details he *hadn't* dreamed about: dragons diving deep in the sea. She paused before adding, 'I also saw Dylan. He was shrouded in darkness, but alive.'

Billy breathed out a huge sigh of relief. He knew Spark's visions could shift and change as quickly as the wind, but it gave him an enormous amount of comfort to know she'd seen Dylan alive. It was a good sign. It was strange that he had shared some of her vision in his dream, but it must have been a coincidence.

'I believe Dylan is close to the sea,' Spark concluded. 'And the city on fire is a more distant vision, one that will happen if we do not find him. If we do not stop the Dragon of Death.'

'We will do everything we can to keep that vision from happening,' said Tank. 'But for now we will continue north and stay by the sea.' He took a deep breath and blew out. Billy braced himself for the heat that came with Tank's fire, but, instead of flames, hot air shot from his mouth so fast it knocked JJ to the ground, shattering the ring of reflection.

Billy and the others climbed onto their dragons, and they all lifted into the sky. The wind whipped Billy's hair and he breathed in the strange scent of lemons from the Forgotten Sea. He felt a renewed sense of purpose and determination. They would find something today. He was sure of it. They had to.

As they flew, he kept his eyes glued to the ground, looking for anything that might give a clue as to where Dylan and Old Gold might be.

Then he saw something that made his blood grow cold. 'Look!' he shouted, pointing.

Far beneath them a dragon lay on its back, its wings bent beneath it at an awkward angle. Even from this far up, Billy could see the blood seeping out from under the dragon's body. And around it grew the putrid purple bushes that Billy associated with dark magic. The sight made him feel sick. It was unnatural and wrong to see a dragon – a powerful dragon – slain like this.

The dragons flew closer together, and Billy sensed their unease echoing his own. 'The Dragon of Death has been here,' said Xing. 'And recently. That is an unnatural death.'

'Is there any sign of my *yeye*?' asked JJ in a strained voice.

'No sign of humans at all,' said Spark gently. 'We should keep going. We have no time to waste.'

They flew on, in tight formation now, and any joy Billy felt from seeing the wonders of this realm evaporated. Seeing the dead dragon had reminded him just how powerful, and how evil, the Dragon of Death was. How would they ever defeat her? They were going to need all the help they could get.

Then an idea struck him. 'Maybe we should ask some of the dragons from this time if they've seen Dylan or Old Gold,' he said. 'Or even the Dragon of Death.'

'We don't know how we will be received,' Xing said. 'It is risky. Especially now the Dragon of Death has made herself known and is taking dragon lives.'

'But it might be a risk we have to take,' said Buttons. 'I was hoping we wouldn't have to interact directly with the dragons of this time, but Billy is right. We need more information. We don't want to wait until it is too late.'

Billy glanced at Buttons and JJ. JJ's face was pale and his whole body tense as he held onto the dragon. Billy felt a surprising rush of pity for him.

'Billy, watch out!' Charlotte shouted from above them. 'Something is heading right towards you!'

Billy straightened up and quickly looked over his shoulder. Flying straight at him, faster even than the dragons, was a pink-and-gold blur. Billy braced himself for impact as it came closer, closer and then . . .

The blur squeaked.

No, the blur *oinked*.

'It's the pig!' cried Billy incredulously. 'It came back!'

'It's so fast!' shouted Ling-Fei.

'And so persistent,' added Xing, sounding less than impressed.

The flying pig was oinking in earnest now, right next to Billy's ear. 'I think it's trying to tell me something!' said Billy. *Spark, slow down*, he thought. Spark gently slowed her pace until she was hovering in mid-air, and the other dragons followed suit. Billy held out his palm and the small pig landed, huffing and puffing as it did.

'Hey, hey, you're okay,' said Billy in a soothing voice, stroking the small pig on its nose. The pig licked his palm. 'What is it?' Billy asked. The pig squeaked again and snorted some more. It kept staring at Billy, and then hopping up and down, almost in excitement.

Billy looked at Ling-Fei and Xing, who were hovering next to him and Spark. 'Ling-Fei, can you try to talk to it? Using your pearl power?' It seemed like too much of a coincidence for the pig to appear a second time. Maybe it was trying to help. And Ling-Fei had the ability to listen to the earth and sense the nearness of living things. She hadn't yet tried to speak to animals, but Billy thought it was worth a shot.

'It is a pig,' said Xing dismissively. 'It cannot speak.'

'And you're a talking dragon,' said Billy curtly.

'I am superior to all other animals, including humans,' Xing snapped back. Billy sighed and again thought about what a strange pairing Ling-Fei, with her gentle demeanour, and Xing, with her spiky attitude, was.

'Billy's right,' said Charlotte. 'We met a creature entirely made out of rocks that could talk. Why not a talking, flying pig?'

'Xing, move closer so I can try to communicate with it,' said Ling-Fei.

'Fine,' grumbled Xing, flying closer to Billy and Spark.

Ling-Fei held her hand out and smiled at the small pig. 'Come here,' she said softly.

The pig looked up at Billy, as if it were asking for permission. Billy grinned and nodded. He liked that the pig had sought him out, whatever the reason. It felt a little like finally getting the dog or cat he'd always wanted. And perhaps the pig really did want to help them.

'I am intrigued by how fast it flies,' said Spark, watching the tiny pig closely as it hopped from Billy's hand to Ling-Fei's. 'It appears to fly as fast as dragons.'

Ling-Fei put her face close to the pig's tiny one and whispered to it. The pig squeaked in return. After a minute, Ling-Fei looked up at the group. 'I don't think my pearl power is developed enough to fully understand all creatures,' she said. 'I'm sorry.'

'Don't be sorry,' said Billy quickly. 'It was worth trying. And your power is awesome.' He gave her what he hoped was a reassuring smile. He felt silly for thinking the pig had some sort of secret message for them. That it was trying to help. Or maybe even warn them about something. He hoped the others couldn't tell how disappointed he was.

'But I did sense something,' Ling-Fei went on. 'I

think the pig wants us to follow it.' She laughed a little, clearly a bit embarrassed. 'I realize that isn't much to go on.'

'It certainly isn't,' said Tank bluntly. 'If we had time to explore this realm, that would be one thing, but we don't. Do not forget Spark's vision.'

'I know!' said Ling-Fei quickly. 'I wasn't saying we should do it, I was just . . . relaying what I sensed.'

'You did well,' said Xing with a sharp glare at Tank.

'Would it be so awful if we *did* follow it?' Billy ventured. He couldn't shake the strange affinity he felt with the tiny pig. He'd trusted his instincts before, with the dragons and with his friends, and it had been the right thing to do. He didn't want to discount the feeling he had now.

'Billy,' Buttons admonished him gently, 'you know we have to stay focused. We all feel the pull to the north, and Spark saw the ocean in her vision. This is the best chance we have of finding them.'

'But . . .' Billy faltered. He still had a strong feeling, deep in his gut, that they should follow the pig, although without a concrete reason he knew he wouldn't be able to convince the others.

'We can't go off on a wild goose chase! Or a tiny pig chase,' said Charlotte firmly. 'Sorry, Billy. We just can't.'

'The pig is welcome to accompany us, if it would like,' said Buttons graciously.

'Did you hear that?' said Ling-Fei to the tiny pig. 'You can come with us.'

The pig squeaked again and flew off her hand towards Billy, landing on his shoulder.

'Now that we've spent enough time with this . . . creature,' said Tank, eyeing it with distaste, 'we should carry on.'

'Wait. I sense dragons,' said Xing suddenly, lifting her head in the air. Xing had the ability to sense magic and life all around her. She inhaled deeply. 'No dark magic, so it isn't the Dragon of Death or any of her followers.'

'Billy,' said Tank, gazing at him, 'while I disagreed with your suggestion to follow the pig, your idea to talk to dragons in this time was a wise one.' He looked at the rest of the group. 'I say we seek these nearby dragons out and ask if they have seen anything. Word of humans travelling on their own in this realm would spread.'

'I agree,' said Spark.

'As long as we continue to go north,' said Buttons, 'I'm happy with this.'

'Hurry,' said Xing, her nose still in the air. 'They are getting out of my range. Follow me!'

The Blast From Below

Billy and the dragons raced through the air. They flew low enough over the Forgotten Sea that Billy felt lemon-scented spray in his face.

Xing led the way, snout up, following the scent of the unfamiliar dragons. 'We are closing in on them,' she called to the rest of the group.

Despite the fact this had been his idea, Billy felt anxious. The last time they'd gone searching for other dragons in the Dragon Realm, back in their own time, it had been a disaster. One that had almost got them killed when they'd encountered Dimitrius, the leader of the nox-wings, the evil dragons who followed the Dragon of Death. Billy hoped these dragons they were looking for now would be friendly. Or, at the very least, not try to kill him and his friends or drain their life force.

Spark, he thought, *should we be worried?*

We should be alert, but not worried, she responded, although Billy didn't get the reassuring *feeling* to match her words. It was strange – usually the sense of whatever Spark was trying to convey came first. Perhaps she was more worried than she was letting on.

He glanced down at the Forgotten Sea and frowned.

The water looked strange, as if it were . . . vibrating. Before he could ask Spark about it, the air itself began to tremble, and a great shuddering blast of sound, high-pitched and keening, ricocheted up from the water. Billy's vision blurred and his ears rang. He felt the sound in his teeth, in his bones.

All the dragons pulled to an abrupt halt, as if the change in the air had stopped them going any further. They hovered, wings beating fast to keep them aloft against the onslaught of noise. Their faces contorted as the air continued to ripple and shudder around them.

The closest feeling Billy had ever had to this was when his brother Eddie had taken him to a concert, and they'd stood right next to a speaker. Billy hadn't known before that day that you could feel sound.

But that was nothing compared to this. His whole body thrummed. With a huge effort, he lifted his hands to cover his ears, but it did nothing. The air quivered with sound waves, so loud and strong that Billy almost thought he could see them. What was going on? Were they being attacked? Had the Dragon of Death found them? Panic gripped Billy's heart.

Finally, just when he thought he couldn't handle it a moment longer and his brain was going to melt, the sound stopped. The air returned to normal. Spark juddered downwards for a quick moment, as if the energy from the sound waves had been keeping her up.

Ears still ringing, Billy looked around. Everyone, even the dragons, was wincing and shaking their heads, as if trying to shake water from their ears.

'What *was* that?' Billy said, or at least he thought

that was what he said. He couldn't actually hear his own voice. He looked in every direction, trying to find the attacker, but his vision was still blurry and he couldn't make out anything past his group.

Slowly sounds came back.

'Battle positions!' commanded Tank, fire flaring from his nostrils.

In an instant, the four dragons swooped together, each one facing a different direction, on the lookout for danger.

All was quiet and no enemies emerged. After a few moments, they relaxed their tight stance, and it felt as if they all let out a collective breath.

'Is everyone all right?' asked Ling-Fei, her voice unsteady.

'That blast of ... whatever it was nearly knocked me off,' JJ rasped. Billy glanced over at him and saw his knuckles were white from how tight he was still clutching Buttons. 'But I'm okay.'

'It felt like a ... supersonic blast or something,' said Charlotte, tilting her head to the side.

'That's what I thought!' Billy jumped in. 'It was so loud it made the air quiver.'

'No sign of what caused it,' said Xing, eyes darting around.

'It felt like it came from ... below us,' said Billy, glancing down at the now-calm waters of the Forgotten Sea.

'There is much we don't know about the Forgotten Sea,' said Spark softly.

'Could it have been the Dragon of Death?' said Billy, looking around warily.

Before anyone could reply, there was a sudden screech from above. Billy looked up and tensed, waiting for another sonic blast. It didn't come. Instead, there was another anguished screech.

'Dragons!' shouted Charlotte.

Two dragons were shooting through the sky, with wings flung back and snouts down. Way above them drifted one of the floating islands that hung in the sky in the Dragon Realm. And below ...

Hurtling down even faster than the diving dragons was a green-and-yellow rock.

Billy realized it wasn't a rock just as Ling-Fei began shouting.

'It's an egg! It's their egg!'

'They won't catch it!' Billy cried. 'They aren't going fast enough!' The dragon egg was about to crash into the Forgotten Sea.

7

A Life For A Life

Billy knew what he had to do.

'Come on, Spark!' he shouted. 'We have to catch it!'

Spark streaked towards the falling egg. *Billy, the egg is falling too fast. Even if we reach it before it crashes into the ocean, we might not be able to catch it at such a speed.*

I saw you catch a star, Billy thought back. *We can catch this egg.*

There was a strange pause from Spark, as if the bond between them had flickered out for a moment. Then it came back, as strong as ever. *The egg might break on impact*, she said.

'We have to try!' Billy shouted out loud. 'Faster!'

With a burst of energy and a powerful flap of Spark's wings, they shot forward.

'We're right behind you, Billy!' Ling-Fei cried out.

'Spark!' Billy said, an idea striking him. 'Remember when Ling-Fei fell off Xing and you used your magic to cushion her fall with water from the lake? Can we try that?'

That should work. But I'll need your help.

Working together through their bond, Spark and Billy shot up a column of water from the Forgotten Sea. At the top, the column unfurled like a flower, ready to catch the egg.

It happened just in time. The egg landed in the water cushion and then Billy and Spark were right beside it. Using his agility pearl power, Billy grabbed the egg with ease, cradling it to his chest.

The egg pulsed against him, and he let out a long breath. He hoped it meant the tiny dragon hatchling inside still lived.

With a flap of wings and a flash of talons, one of the dragons who had been chasing the egg careered into Spark. 'Give me my egg!'

The dragon was a vivid yellow, with wide wings and

a long, sinuous neck. Its sharp claws glistened like knives in the sunlight. Claws that came perilously close to Billy's exposed neck. Spark threw her wings up to shield him and reared in the air, electricity crackling all around her.

'Watch yourself, yellow-scale,' she said.

Xing, Tank and Buttons, their humans still astride their backs, flanked Spark and Billy. Tank let out a warning rumble.

'I do not fear you!' screamed the yellow dragon. 'I would face death itself for my egg.' The other dragon, this one green, with a huge head and giant horns, swooped in next to the yellow dragon. It blew out a stream of billowing smoke.

Billy realized that these new dragons might not take the time to ask questions before they attacked.

'Wait!' he yelled, wanting to explain.

'We were trying to help!' cried out Ling-Fei. 'We don't want to fight you!'

'Speak for yourself,' muttered Charlotte. 'I know an attack stance when I see one.' She bared her teeth from her perch atop Tank's head. 'Stand down!'

'We don't want to hurt you, or your egg,' said Billy

quickly before things escalated further. 'Here.' He nudged Spark forward and then offered the egg.

In a flash, the yellow dragon had it ensconced in its wings. The bright green dragon nuzzled the egg and then looked up at Billy. 'You were not trying to steal our egg?'

Billy shook his head. 'We saw it falling and caught it before it sank into the ocean. We were trying to help.'

'Thank you,' the green dragon said finally in a raspy voice. 'We owe you a great debt.'

The yellow dragon looked up. Its long tongue flicked out of the side of its mouth, as if it were contemplating something. 'I am sure you can understand my reaction,' it said. 'A mother's instincts, you know.'

Hearing the word 'mother' gave Billy a tight feeling in his chest. His mother had no idea where he was right now or how much danger he was in, but she probably knew that he was missing from camp. He swallowed the lump that appeared in his throat. He missed her, and his dad, and his brother, with a sudden fierceness. He hoped he would see them again after all this. He reminded himself that the reason they wanted to stop the Dragon of Death in the first place was to protect both realms. He was doing this to protect his family.

'I'm not a mother,' he said, feeling awkward. 'But I understand. My mom would be the same way.'

The yellow dragon gave him a sharp-toothed grin. 'Wise for a hatchling. And it appears *you* are the one we should be thanking.'

Billy ducked his head. 'It was all of us,' he said.

'No,' said the green dragon. 'We saw. It was you, you dived on your dragon.' He eyed Spark. 'You must be heart-bonded. A rare thing indeed. And I've never seen a dragon of your kind before.'

'We aren't from . . . here,' said Spark slowly.

'We were hoping to talk to you,' added Buttons. 'We sensed you nearby and were coming to find you when your egg fell.'

Ling-Fei gave a little gasp. 'The blast! Was that what made your egg fall?'

'Indeed,' said the bright green dragon. 'A blast like that has not been heard or felt in many years.' He looked at the yellow dragon, who was still cradling the egg. 'We weren't prepared. We were on our island.' He glanced up at the floating island far above them. 'Our egg was snug in its nest when the tremors in the air knocked it loose. We didn't notice the egg had fallen until it was too late.'

'It would have been too late if it wasn't for you,' said the yellow dragon. 'I am glad you had a reason to seek us.' She narrowed her eyes. 'You are not the first creatures we've seen recently that are "not from here", as you say.'

Billy bolted straight up. 'My friend, he's missing, he was kidnapped!' His words spilled out all on top of each other.

Hush, Spark thought, harsher than she usually was. *We do not want to tell them the reasons we are here.*

'I hear word of a human hatchling, with an old man, walking on foot through our lands,' said the green dragon slowly.

Billy nearly fell off Spark in excitement. *Stay calm*, Spark thought. Billy noticed JJ was sitting up and leaning forward too. He knew JJ must have been worried about Old Gold.

'Do you know where they are?' said Xing.

'They were last seen heading north,' said the green dragon. 'Beyond the fire marshes.'

Billy let out a massive breath. They had been going the right way. *We're coming, Dylan*, he thought as hard as he could, as if maybe his friend could hear him across the realm. *We're coming! Just hold on a little longer!* And then he got nervous. The fire marshes? What were those? They sounded like something Dylan would find terrifying. Especially if he was travelling on foot with Old Gold.

'That is very helpful,' said Tank. 'But we have another question for you.'

'Is it about the dragon who brings a dark and terrible magic to our land?' said the yellow dragon, holding her egg even closer.

'Yes,' said Billy, making his voice as strong as he could. 'We're looking for that dragon too.'

'We have not come across her, and hope to keep it that way,' said the yellow dragon. 'She has been slaying dragons that don't join her. Join her for what, I do not know. But she is seeking followers. They call themselves the Noxious.' She paused. 'The magic she brings is potent, and the power she offers is tempting. But any dragon who takes life so easily is one I want to stay far away from.'

Billy gulped, the relief he had felt at hearing Dylan was alive quickly fading to terror.

'Have many joined her?' asked Buttons gravely.

'It is unclear,' said the green dragon. 'We only know what we have heard.'

'She's building an army of nox-wings in this time,' said Tank grimly.

'In this time versus what other?' said the yellow dragon.

'It is a long story,' said Buttons. 'I'm afraid telling you the whole thing would take more time than we have. But thank you for sharing what you know.'

'One last question,' said Spark. 'Do you know where this new dragon has been seen?'

The green dragon's eyes clouded. 'There have been sightings of dark magic across the realm. This dragon you seek seems to be on the move. But she is not near here as far as I know.'

'The sooner we find her, the better,' said Xing.

'We're still going to find Dylan and Old Gold first, right?' said Billy, panic blooming in his chest.

'Of course,' said Buttons. 'Not only because of how much we want to be reunited with Dylan, but also because it would not be wise for us to go into battle against the Dragon of Death unless we were at full strength. Without Dylan, I am not as strong as I can be.' He glanced at JJ. 'Please do not take offence.'

'I don't,' said JJ, and he sounded as if he meant it. Billy was starting to think JJ wasn't as bad as he had always thought.

'Do y'all know what caused that blast?' said Charlotte. 'We worried it might have been the Dragon of Death herself, but, from what you've said, it couldn't have been.'

'Strange,' said the yellow dragon. 'I thought all knew of the Screaming Serpent.'

'The what?' said Billy.

'The Screaming Serpent was once one of us, a dragon that flew in the sky and sea – until it made a terrible trade with the guardian of the Forgotten Sea. It offered its wings, its flight, in return for a great treasure. And it received the treasure, but not only were its wings ripped off, it was chained to the sea floor. All it has now is its treasure to keep it company.

And, if anything comes near the Screaming Serpent, it screams. Something must have come very close for us to hear it scream like that.'

'But that sound has not been heard for centuries,' said the green dragon. 'The Screaming Serpent is in the deepest, darkest part of the Forgotten Sea. To even dive down to those depths would be risking one's life.'

'That sound came from the *bottom* of the sea?' said Charlotte. 'I'm sure glad we weren't any closer!'

Billy swallowed. What creature would be strong enough, reckless enough to dive to the bottom of the sea and face that terrible sound head-on? Could it have been the Dragon of Death? Could the treasure the Screaming Serpent guarded be one of the pearls?

'I have heard legends of this creature, even in our time,' Spark said slowly. She shook her head. 'But, as much as I would love to find out more, we must keep moving. We don't have time to waste.'

'Before you go, I have something for you,' said the yellow dragon, locking eyes with Billy. 'You saved our egg. You saved a life. And I do not want to be in that debt.'

'We do not believe in the old ways,' said Buttons quickly. 'You do not owe us at all.'

'Perhaps you do not believe in the old ways, but the old ways are *our* ways. And so it must be done.'

Billy swallowed. The anticipation was making him nervous. '*What* must be done?'

'A life for a life,' said the yellow dragon.

She opened her mouth wide, showing all her teeth, and Billy saw something glinting on her tongue.

Hold out your palm, Spark whispered in his head.

Billy held out his open hand, willing it not to shake.

Using her long tongue, the yellow dragon dropped a glinting gold coin in Billy's palm. It landed with a wet thud.

The coin had deep scratches all over it, and it was heavier than it looked. As Billy inspected it, the scratches shimmered, and an eye stared back at him. Then the light shifted, and the eye was gone.

'That's . . . weird,' he said.

Spark gasped. 'A soul coin.'

'What's a soul coin?' said Billy, turning it over.

The green dragon let out a short laugh. 'What it sounds like. There is a soul trapped in that coin.'

'*What?*' Billy nearly dropped it.

'A life for a life,' said the yellow dragon. 'Now I owe you nothing.'

'What do you mean, "there is a soul trapped in that coin"?' said Ling-Fei, alarm etched across her face. 'Whose soul?'

'The soul of one of my enemies, of course,' said the yellow dragon, sounding vaguely bored. 'Dragon, not human, if that makes a difference to you.'

Billy slipped the coin into Dylan's backpack. He didn't want it staring at him. 'Um, thank you,' he said.

'A life for a life,' the yellow dragon repeated.

Unexpected Gifts

'Is there *really* a soul trapped inside that coin?' Billy asked, feeling mildly alarmed by the whole thing. 'Like, really, *really*? It isn't just a saying? Or maybe a joke?'

They'd said goodbye to the yellow and green dragons and were flying further north along the coast, keeping an eye out for signs of Old Gold and Dylan, or the Dragon of Death. Billy felt as if it were a race between them and the Dragon of Death to see who would find Old Gold and Dylan first. Knowing that the Dragon of Death was building up an army of nox-wings in this time made her all the more dangerous and Billy knew they had to do everything they could to stop her before she grew even more powerful.

At least they knew for sure now that Old Gold and Dylan were alive and in this time. That gave Billy a rush of hope. But right now he was finding it hard to focus on anything other than the soul coin he carried with him. 'Is there really an actual soul in it?' he went on. He shuddered, remembering how the coin had blinked at him.

Spark sighed and Billy sensed a slight tinge of frustration in her. 'Yes,' she said. 'As I've said. The soul coin has a soul in it. There is not much more I can say about it.'

'Isn't that cruel?' Billy half wanted to throw the entire backpack into the sea below. It made his skin crawl thinking about a soul trapped in there, hitching a ride.

'You heard the dragon,' said Tank, who was next to them. They were flying in tight formation, close enough to be able to speak. 'The soul belonged to one of her enemies.'

'And this isn't dark magic?' said Billy dubiously.

'The soul would have known the stakes,' added

Buttons. 'If I recall correctly, during this time it was common for dragons to bargain their souls in battle. It became less fashionable after a while.'

'Gee, I wonder why,' Charlotte deadpanned.

They flew on and on. As each hour passed, Billy's hopes that they would find Dylan began to fade. The dragons they'd spoken to hadn't even seen Dylan and Old Gold with their own eyes, they'd only heard of sightings. That didn't mean Dylan was still alive.

It had been a long day of flying, and Billy could tell the dragons were getting tired. They would have to rest again soon. The coast stretched on and on endlessly, with nothing to suggest they were any closer to finding their friend. To make matters worse, they saw more slain dragons, and the strange purple plants that grew in the presence of dark magic were appearing ever more frequently. Billy couldn't be sure, but it also looked as if the sky was beginning to take on a red tint, as it had in the Dragon Realm of their time when dark magic was at its height. He pushed his fear aside and tried to focus on looking for Dylan.

Something squeaked next to his ear. He turned quickly, on high alert, and then started to laugh.

It was the tiny flying pig. 'Where have you been?' Billy said affectionately. The pig flew fast, its small gold wings whirring soundlessly, and it kept up with the dragons easily. Billy held out a hand for it and the pig landed gently on his palm, wriggling around. Billy laughed again. 'Hey, that tickles!'

Then something caught his eye. A glint of silver around one of the pig's tiny hooves. Almost like . . . a ring.

Billy looked closer. No, not almost like a ring. Exactly like a ring.

The tiny pig was wearing a ring.

And not just any ring. A ring he had seen before. A silver Claddagh ring.

A silver Claddagh ring that Billy had last seen on Dylan O'Donnell.

Billy remembered when he'd first noticed the ring. It was hard to miss. In the centre of the ring were two hands holding a heart with a crown on top. He remembered asking Dylan why he wore a ring and Dylan had looked at his hand, almost as if he'd forgotten it was there.

'Oh! This is my Claddagh ring,' he'd said. As if that explained it. 'It's a Galway thing. My granddad gave me this one when I started secondary school.'

'Why has it got . . . so much stuff on it?' said Billy.

Dylan laughed. 'It's just what they look like. The hands represent friendship. The heart represents love. And the crown is for loyalty. My mam and dad both wear one. Everyone I know does. I never take mine off.'

And here was that ring, with the hands, the heart and the crown, glinting on the pig's foot. Billy gently pulled the ring off the pig.

'What's that?' said Charlotte, looking across at him.

'It's Dylan's Claddagh ring,' said Billy, his throat tight. He'd been so happy to see it at first, before he realized what this might mean. If Dylan didn't have his ring on . . .

It was the worst outcome.

He felt cold all over. This was it. They'd failed. Dylan was gone and never coming back. Billy hung his head, overwhelmed with sadness and guilt. They were too late.

'He's not dead,' said Buttons, realizing what he

was thinking as he flew closer to inspect the ring. 'I'd know. I would feel it. That's how the bond works. If anything, we're getting closer.'

'Then why does this pig have his ring?' Billy burst out. He couldn't shake the dread that something terrible had happened to Dylan. But if Buttons was saying he still felt Dylan through the bond . . . a tiny kernel of hope lit up in Billy.

'Maybe Dylan dropped it,' suggested Charlotte.

Billy shook his head. 'He never takes it off.'

'Maybe . . .' Ling-Fei said, watching the pig closely. The pig was flitting around in excitement. 'Maybe this time he did. Maybe he took it off and gave it to the pig! As a message!'

Billy stared at the ring. Then stared at the pig. Was that possible?

'Ling-Fei,' he said slowly. 'Didn't you say yesterday that you got the sense the pig wanted us to follow it?'

'Yes!' said Ling-Fei, excited now. 'And it still does! More than ever.'

Billy looked up at the dragons, who were also staring at the tiny squeaking pig and the ring sitting in Billy's hand.

'Quite a day for unexpected gifts,' said Xing.

'Can we follow the pig?' Billy asked. 'I know before it seemed ridiculous, but now . . .' He let his voice trail off. And then he came to a decision. He cleared his throat and said firmly, 'I'm going to follow the pig. I'd rather you all came with me. But I'll walk by myself if I have to. I think Ling-Fei's right, and I don't want to miss this chance.'

'Of course we won't let you go by yourself,' said Charlotte, tossing her long blonde hair over her shoulder. 'We're coming with you. Right, Ling-Fei?'

'Right,' said Ling-Fei.

'I agree,' added JJ unexpectedly. Billy gave him a tentative smile in appreciation. JJ nodded back.

'All of you?' said Billy to the dragons.

'I, too, would like to follow the pig,' said Buttons.

'Never would have thought I'd be following you around so much,' said JJ wryly. 'Or following a pig anywhere.'

'I both applaud your loyalty and frown at your foolishness. Go on foot? You'd be eaten by sunset,' said Xing. She flashed her diamond teeth in a sharp smile. 'The small pig does seem to know something.'

Billy was filled with a renewed sense of hope and determination. 'Spark, you agree with me, right?' he said, realizing that his dragon had stayed quiet.

'I will go where you go,' said Spark.

Billy looked at the flying pig. 'Lead the way, little piggy!' With a high-pitched oink, the pig flew inland, and the dragons followed.

The pig led them away from the coast. Away from the Forgotten Sea.

They were still flying roughly north, but at more of a diagonal. North-west.

Billy was glad. He thought the dragons might not have continued following if the pig had headed south, somewhere completely different from what Buttons sensed, and what they'd heard from the dragons they had met.

The pig kept pausing so they could catch up. Billy could tell it rankled the dragons' pride that this small pig was faster than them. But the pig's speed and eagerness gave Billy confidence. Maybe it really had found Dylan. He couldn't bear to think of the alternative: that it was leading them further from Dylan, or, even worse, leading them into a trap. He had to hold onto the hope that they would find Dylan, and soon. He felt almost light-headed with nerves and excitement. *Dylan, we're coming*, he thought.

Finally, just as the sun started to set and the three moons grew brighter against the darkening sky, the small flying pig began to slow down.

Billy frantically scanned the ground. Where was he? Where was Dylan?

He didn't see any humans. He didn't see anything at all except a large, solitary tree with a thick trunk and gnarled roots sprouting out from the ground. The tree had no leaves, and its long, spindly branches appeared to be reaching for the sky. Reaching towards them.

The pig stopped above the tree, and hovered and squeaked.

'There isn't anything here,' said Billy, frustration making his voice sharp.

'Except for that super-creepy tree,' said JJ.

'The tree ... isn't a normal tree,' said Ling-Fei slowly, a look of concentration on her face. Billy realized she was using her power to tune into the natural world. 'I think we should inspect it more closely.'

'I feel a strong pull towards the tree,' said Buttons, staring down at it.

'It gives me the heebie-jeebies,' said Charlotte with a shudder. 'And look, some of those creepy purple plants are growing at the base.'

'We should be careful,' said Billy. He remembered what had happened the last time he'd underestimated plant life in the Dragon Realm. He'd ended up unconscious.

The dragons landed in a semicircle a safe distance from the tree. But the flying pig flew right up to it, going round and round, squeaking. It looked as if it was trying to talk to the tree.

'I hope this has not been a fool's errand,' said Xing, eyeing the pig with distaste. 'You have put a lot of faith in this small swine. That tree stinks of dark magic.'

Billy slid off Spark's back and landed in a crouch on the ground. 'I'm going to take a look,' he said. He held the ring clenched tightly in his fist.

'Billy, wait!' cried Ling-Fei, running up behind him. 'Something is strange about this tree. I sense dark magic in it but something else too. Something I can't quite figure out. Be careful!'

Billy crept up to the tree, waiting for something to happen.

The tree stood silently. The pig continued to squeak. The dragons watched.

Billy sighed. He took the ring and held it out to the pig. 'This! I want to find the owner of this!' he yelled up to it. 'Where did you get the ring?'

'I gave the ring to the pig!' cried the tree.

Billy jumped back.

'It's me!' the tree cried again. 'It's me, Dylan!'

The Voice From The Tree

Billy's mouth dropped open.

He took a step back.

'Hello?' the voice came again. It actually did sound like Dylan. Billy's heart began to hammer in his chest. What was going on? Had they really found Dylan? Or was this some sort of dark-magic trick?

Billy wasn't sure when Charlotte and Ling-Fei had moved up beside him, but there they were on either side. He glanced over his shoulder at JJ, who was hanging back, and nodded, inviting him to join them. JJ stood hesitantly next to Charlotte. Billy felt like it was important JJ was here. After all, he was a part of this rescue mission now. The tiny pig flitted round them in increasing excitement.

'Dylan?' Billy said incredulously. And then again, a little louder, 'Dylan! It's Billy! Can you hear me?'

'Billy!' came Dylan's voice. 'Oh, wow, I am so glad to hear you.'

It was definitely Dylan's voice. There was no question about that.

'Dylan! Dylan!' Buttons ran at full tilt towards the tree, nearly knocking Billy over. 'DYLAN!' Buttons cried again, throwing his short arms as far as they'd go round the tree. 'You're alive! I'm so glad you're alive! I've missed you so much. It's been torture being separated!'

'Buttons!' Dylan's voice hitched. 'I thought I could sense you coming closer, but I wasn't sure if I was imagining it. I've missed you too.'

Billy stepped closer to the tree. 'I'm glad you're alive too but ...' He cleared his throat. 'Did Old Gold turn you into a tree?'

There was a pause. 'Come on, Billy. You're smarter than that,' said the tree in Dylan's voice. 'I'm stuck *in* the tree. I'm not the tree.'

'I knew you weren't the tree!' yelled Charlotte. 'Obviously you are stuck in the tree.'

'Could have said something,' said Billy under his breath, but he was smiling. 'I can't believe we found you!' he said louder, so Dylan could hear him.

'Dylan, are you okay?' asked Ling-Fei.

'I'm alive,' said Dylan, and his voice sounded older than Billy remembered it. 'I'm alive, and you guys are here. But . . . I'm stuck inside a tree. So I've been better.'

'We will get you out, of course!' said Buttons. He looked at the other dragons. 'A tree is no match for us.' His claws extended like a cat's, razor-sharp and deadly. 'Dylan, get back!'

Buttons lifted his arm up and struck the trunk with his claws.

But they didn't even make a dent. He cleared his throat and laughed a little. 'Give me a minute,' he said and began to drag his claws down the trunk with an ear-piercing screech.

Billy had never really thought about what nails on a chalkboard might sound like, but he was sure it was a million times better than this.

The tree remained unscathed.

Anxiety began to gnaw at Billy. What if they couldn't get Dylan out? How could they come all this way only for him to be trapped for ever? They had to be able to open the tree, they just had to. And fast. Because where was Old Gold? He must have been nearby. And probably coming back any moment.

Buttons cleared his throat. 'This tree seems to be stronger than a normal tree.'

'It is clearly enchanted by dark magic,' said Xing, sniffing with displeasure. 'Are we sure it really is Dylan inside and this isn't a trap?'

'Of course it is Dylan!' said Buttons, sounding outraged by the mere suggestion it might not be. 'Are you suggesting I might not recognize my own human?'

'It really is me!' shouted Dylan from inside the tree. 'If it wasn't, would I know that Billy has a brother named Eddie? And that Charlotte was Little Miss of the South? And that you, Xing, think Ling-Fei has the heart of a poet?'

'I suppose it really is Dylan,' said Xing. 'In that

case, we must move fast.' She looked behind her. 'I'll stay on the lookout for Old Gold or any nox-wings. In the meantime, one of you must figure out how to open that tree. And quickly.'

'Let me try!' said Charlotte. Her pearl power gave her incredible strength. Billy had seen her toss boulders as if they were pebbles, and once she'd thrown him like a javelin. If anyone was going to be able to open the tree with brute strength, it was Charlotte.

'Wait!' Dylan sounded panicked. 'What's Charlotte going to do?'

'Hold on, Dylan!' said Charlotte, and then she took a mighty swing at the tree. Her fist connected with the tree with a dull thud.

'Son of a biscuit eater!' Charlotte said, shaking out her hand and inspecting it. 'That hurt!' She looked over her shoulder at Tank. 'Tank, I think this has gotta be you.'

'Step aside, children,' said Tank. They moved quickly out of the way as Tank took a few thundering steps towards the tree. The ground shook beneath them.

'Do be careful,' said Buttons, looking nervous.

Tank raised himself up to his full height. He was twice as tall as the tree. He leaned down, gripped it in his fist and pulled.

And pulled.

And pulled.

Smoke poured out of his nostrils with the effort.

Billy had never seen Tank strain himself, and it was incredibly awkward. After a few more torturous moments, he stopped and stared down at the tree.

'I probably shouldn't blast fire at it, should I?' Tank mused.

'NO!' yelled Buttons, Billy and Dylan from inside the tree.

Billy leaned against the tree. 'Dylan, we'll get you out. I promise.'

'If everyone is done with their ridiculous attempts to open the tree, I have some questions for the boy,' said Xing, twining round the tree. 'First. How did you get in it in the first place?'

'Old Gold locked me in here.'

'He is powerful enough to do that?' said Buttons incredulously.

'He is now.' Dylan paused and then his voice broke a little bit as he added, 'He did it. He found the Dragon of Death.'

Never Meant To Be Friends

The news hit Billy like a physical blow. He stumbled back, clutching his stomach. Of course they had known Old Gold was seeking the Dragon of Death, but he had thought perhaps they might be able to stop the two from meeting. Now that they were together, they would be more powerful than ever before, and much more difficult to defeat.

'No,' Billy whispered. Behind him, the dragons hissed and Tank let out a roar of frustration.

Billy was glad they had found Dylan, but he desperately wished they had been here earlier. That they had found him and Old Gold before the Dragon of Death had. Now it meant they were edging closer and closer to the vision that Spark had seen – the vision they were working so hard to keep from becoming a reality.

'Yeah, it's pretty bad,' said Dylan, as if he had heard Billy's thoughts. 'And to make things even worse –' Billy didn't think it *could* get much worse – 'the Dragon of Death had a pearl. So now Old Gold has a power too.'

'Where are they?' thundered Tank. 'And why have they left you locked in a tree?'

'I wish I knew the answers to those questions,' said Dylan. 'All I know is they've gone off to do something and are coming back here to get me.' He paused. 'Apparently, the Dragon of Death has plans for me. I don't think they are pleasant ones.'

Even though he couldn't see him, Billy could perfectly picture Dylan's expression as he said this. He felt a sudden rush of happiness in spite of everything.

'It isn't all bad,' said Spark, echoing Billy's thoughts. 'We've found you. And we'll get you out and be gone before they return.' She spoke with a calm confidence. And she was right. They'd found Dylan! They'd deal with the rest once they'd figured out how to release him from this tree.

'Maybe I can talk to the tree,' said Ling-Fei, coming up to it. She crouched low by the roots and whispered.

'I always thought she was weird, but this is next level,' muttered JJ.

'Will you please shut up?' said Charlotte with a threatening glare.

JJ took a step back. The fragile connection Billy had felt between himself, Charlotte, Ling-Fei and JJ seemed to falter. It was almost like a spiderweb breaking. But he couldn't worry about that now. They had to free Dylan before Old Gold and the Dragon of Death returned.

After a few moments, Ling-Fei stood up, shaking her head. 'It isn't a natural tree,' she said. 'I can sense its life, and Dylan inside, but nothing more. I'm sorry to be so useless.'

'That isn't useless,' said Xing. 'Now we know it *really* is Dylan in there, and not an imposter.'

'Excuse me,' huffed Buttons. 'We've already been

over this! I would have been able to tell if it was an imposter!'

Xing shrugged. 'It is good to have it confirmed.'

'We don't have time for this!' Billy said loudly. He could feel the minutes slipping away and was sure that at any moment the Dragon of Death herself would be on them. 'We have to stay focused!'

'Billy is right,' said Spark. She paused before adding, 'We must hurry. We are not prepared yet to face the Dragon of Death. We need to find the rest of the pearls. We might have been able to take her on before she bonded with Old Gold, but now her powers will be magnified and she will be more dangerous than ever. We cannot risk being ambushed by her. We must leave here, and soon.'

JJ stepped up to the tree. 'Hey, Dylan,' he said.

'Is that JJ? You guys brought JJ? What is going on out there? Have I been replaced?'

'That is what you're worried about?' said Charlotte. 'And of course you haven't been replaced. JJ could never replace you.'

JJ's face hardened. Charlotte faltered when she

saw his expression. 'Sorry, JJ,' she said. 'You know what I mean.'

'Yeah, I do,' said JJ, and Billy knew that JJ was choosing to think it meant that Charlotte – and Billy and Ling-Fei and probably the dragons – hated him. Even though Billy knew that Charlotte had really only meant that Dylan was irreplaceable. He wanted to say something but didn't know what, and he had a suspicion that no matter what he said, JJ wouldn't believe him.

JJ moved closer to the tree and spoke again. 'So my *yeye* is still alive?' he said.

'I mean, last I saw him, yes. But that was when the Dragon of Death was flying towards us.' Dylan paused. 'I didn't see her up close – she was still so far away in the sky – but the feeling I got from her presence was terrible. The worst thing I've ever felt in my whole life. My stomach started to hurt and my vision went fuzzy, as if I'd been poisoned or something. At first, I thought it was just nerves, but then the bad feeling overwhelmed me and I blacked out. The next thing I knew, I woke up in this tree.'

'How sure are you that they're coming back?' said JJ.

Dylan sighed so loudly it was audible through the tree trunk. 'Because, when I woke up in the tree, I heard them talking about it. They've been gone for hours now.'

JJ leaned his hands against the tree. 'I'm sorry for ... everything my *yeye* has done,' he whispered.

The tree began to glow beneath JJ's hands. He jumped back. A loud crack echoed through the air, and the tree began to move.

'Dylan! The tree is moving!' shouted Billy. What was happening?

'I know! I can feel it in here!' said Dylan, sounding panicked.

'JJ, what did you do?' said Billy.

JJ shook his head, his face ashen. 'I don't know! I just touched it!'

'The tree recognizes you,' said Xing. 'Your grandfather must have locked it with his blood, and of course you share blood with him.'

With a great creak, the tree bent over, like a very tall man bending at the waist, and its long branches moved forward like many arms. The branches turned towards the trunk and pulled it open, as if opening a coat.

Dylan fell out.

Buttons moved faster than Billy had ever seen. He scooped up Dylan and whisked him from the tree, far from the reaching branches and the now gaping opening in the trunk. It seemed to be breathing.

'Move away from the tree!' said Tank to the others. 'It will be waiting for a body to fill it.'

Everyone quickly took a few steps back – everyone but JJ, who stood, staring.

'Dylan!' cried Billy as he and Charlotte and Ling-Fei ran towards their friend. Buttons gently placed Dylan on the ground and stood back to let Billy and the others by. Dylan swayed on his feet for a moment but then Billy, Charlotte and Ling-Fei embraced him in a group hug. Billy was overwhelmed with the fact that they'd done it. They'd found Dylan. He was alive and whole and with them.

'I can't believe you guys are here!' said Dylan, his voice cracking. 'I thought I was a goner.'

'You should never have doubted us,' said Charlotte, her eyes shining with unshed tears.

'Let me see my human properly!' said Buttons, pushing Billy and Charlotte out of the way.

'Buttons, I am so glad to see you,' said Dylan, and the dragon and the boy hugged. Buttons looked as if he was about to cry.

'And I'm so glad you're back,' said Buttons.

'Hey, you guys,' said JJ.

Something in his voice made Billy look up.

'What is it?' Billy said. 'You should move away from the tree. You heard Tank.'

But JJ was still staring at the opening in the tree. 'I know you came here to find Dylan. And I'm glad you did. I really appreciate you making sure I didn't get killed in this place. And I've actually sort of enjoyed myself.' He laughed a little, but it was a sad laugh. Then he sighed. 'I know you are all mad at my *yeye*.'

Billy started to get a sinking feeling in his stomach.

JJ went on. 'But he's why I came with you. To find him. And I haven't yet. So I'm going to wait here for him.'

He looked up and smiled at Billy. 'And you aren't the big losers I thought you were. You're actually all pretty cool.' Then, before Billy could fully comprehend what JJ was doing, he stepped inside the tree.

'JJ!' shouted Billy, lunging forward.

The tree closed itself quickly, melding together seamlessly, and then straightened.

It was as if it had never opened. Except that now it had a different boy inside it.

'JJ! Get out here!' Billy demanded, banging on the trunk. 'This isn't funny!'

'I'm not trying to be funny,' said JJ. 'This is what I want. And I think, deep down, it is what you all want too. There isn't a dragon for me now. And the four of you have your special magic powers and magic bond. You don't need me.'

'Don't be like that! Of course we need you,' said Charlotte, and as she said it Billy realized it was true. Sure, at the start he hadn't wanted JJ with them, and he'd even unfairly blamed him for what had happened, but JJ was one of them now.

'Jin Jié Jūn, please come out,' said Ling-Fei, approaching the tree. Billy realized he had never heard JJ's full name before. 'We want you to come with us.'

'I've been doing what you all want since we went through that portal. Now I'm doing what I want to do. And what I want is to wait here for my *yeye*. And I know if I wasn't inside this tree, one of your dragons would pick me up and make me go with you. This way we all get what we want. You get Dylan. I get to be reunited with my *yeye*. Don't worry about me. I can get myself out if I need to,' said JJ from inside the tree.

'It's true,' said Spark gently. 'If this is what the boy wants, we cannot force him out of the tree. And we should not wait here much longer.' She turned her gaze on Dylan. 'Dylan, you said you heard Old Gold and the Dragon of Death earlier. Did they say anything about where they might be going?'

Dylan scrunched his eyes tight, clearly trying to remember. Billy was amazed he still had his glasses. 'Something about . . . the sea? Seashells? Wait, that's not it. Maybe coral?'

'The Coral Pearl,' said Xing. 'They've gone for the Coral Pearl.'

Several things slotted into place in Billy's mind all at once, like multiple keys being played on the piano to make a chord. 'Didn't the dragons we met earlier say that the Screaming Serpent was protecting treasure? Could it have been protecting ... the Coral Pearl?'

'That's it,' breathed Spark. 'The Dragon of Death is searching for the rest of the pearls. She already had the Flaming Pearl from when we first banished her, and now she will have the Coral Pearl too.'

'Billy,' said Xing, 'it pains me to admit this, but I'm impressed. We should have made the connection about the Coral Pearl as soon as we felt the blast. Well done,' she added begrudgingly.

'But why didn't we sense the Dragon of Death?' said Ling-Fei.

'The Forgotten Sea is very, very deep,' said Xing. 'Even though we were able to hear the Screaming Serpent, we wouldn't have been able to sense the Dragon of Death. Which means, luckily for us, she wouldn't have sensed us either.'

Billy shivered at the thought of the Dragon of Death being right beneath them.

'But that was hours ago!' said Charlotte. 'They could be back any minute! And Spark said we aren't prepared.'

'The pearls,' said Spark. 'We have to find the

rest of the pearls before they do. If the Dragon of Death finds the remaining pearls, there may be no stopping her.'

'We can't just leave JJ in the tree,' said Billy. He was reeling from everything that had happened. He had been so focused on finding Dylan, he hadn't fully thought about what would come next. Spark was right – they had to find the remaining pearls now. Especially if the Dragon of Death had both the Flaming Pearl and the Coral Pearl. He knew they had to get out of here. But it felt wrong to leave JJ.

'He gives us no choice,' said Tank. 'He has put himself in there, and only he can get himself out.'

'But, JJ . . . you know we're going to be battling the Dragon of Death,' said Billy slowly. 'And if you are with Old Gold . . .' The implications of this struck him suddenly. JJ could tell Old Gold and the Dragon of Death everything that Billy and his friends were planning. Billy had thought he could trust JJ, that they were even starting to be friends, but now he wasn't so sure.

'We were never meant to be friends, Billy Chan,'

said JJ. 'But it was nice hanging out with you for a while. Now get out of here. I mean it.'

'Billy,' said Spark urgently. 'We must leave. Quickly.'

'Thanks for getting me out,' Dylan called to JJ as he clambered on Buttons. 'Even if it wasn't on purpose, thank you.'

'We must go. Now,' said Spark, scanning the skies. 'We need to be far from here.'

Billy felt an unexpected lump in his throat. 'See you . . . soon. I guess,' he said to the tree with JJ inside it.

There was no response. With a surprisingly heavy heart, Billy climbed onto Spark's back as his friends did the same with their dragons. They were reunited with Dylan, and it felt good and right, but it was not how Billy had imagined it. They took off into the sky, leaving JJ and the tree behind.

The Floating Island

Billy kept looking back over his shoulder at the tree with JJ inside. He watched it get smaller and smaller, until he couldn't see it at all.

'I did not realize you had become friends,' said Spark gently as they flew through the night sky, stars twinkling around them. They flew behind the others, far enough back that they could speak without being heard but close enough for safety.

'I didn't either,' said Billy. 'But I guess we had.' He paused. 'And, even if we weren't friends, I still feel bad just ... leaving him like that.'

'Loyal, strong, brave and true,' said Spark. 'You have proven time and again that you four were meant to open the mountain. That you were meant to save us all.'

Billy sighed, and he felt as if the night air sighed in response as it whipped his hair back. 'Sometimes I think we just made things worse. If we hadn't opened the mountain, Dylan would have never been taken, and JJ wouldn't be stuck in the tree right now. We'd still be at camp. Safe. Our parents would know where we were. Everything would be fine.'

'Billy,' said Spark gently. 'You know that isn't true. The Dragon of Death would have arrived in our time. And, with the nox-wings, she would have gone into your realm. Your world would be at war. Nobody would be safe.'

'I don't know,' said Billy slowly. 'You've said dragons have almost infinite knowledge about both realms, but how much do you know about human weapons? We have, like . . . a lot. A lot of big, scary weapons. Things that could probably take down a dragon. Even the Dragon of Death.'

'I am familiar with the weapons you speak of,' said Spark. 'I have seen them in visions. Do you think that would save the realms, Billy Chan? Bombs? The violence would be unending.'

'I guess you're right,' said Billy. But still, guilt trailed him like a shadow.

'And, I must admit, I am personally very happy you opened the mountain. Otherwise we'd still be stuck in there,' said Spark, and Billy smiled.

'I'm glad about that too,' he said, but then his smile faltered. 'I just wish that nobody had to be stuck anywhere.'

'JJ chose to go into that tree,' Spark said. 'He knew what he was doing.'

'I feel like he betrayed us,' Billy said, the thought only just occurring to him. 'Like he was on our team, and then . . . he wasn't.'

'Betrayal is a strong word, Billy,' said Spark. 'You do not yet know what JJ may or may not do.'

'But you do, right? In your visions?'

'I wish my visions were that clear,' said Spark. 'You know I only see flashes. Sometimes feelings. I have not seen JJ.'

A cold feeling slithered through Billy. 'I hope that doesn't mean he . . . doesn't make it.'

'We will either see him again or we will not. Either way, you will be unhappy with the outcome. It is better to put him out of your mind. We have other things to focus on.'

Billy was surprised at how callous Spark sounded, but maybe that was just how dragons were. For all they understood about humans, they still *weren't* human. Not at all. And it wasn't just their scales and tails and magic. It was more than that. Sometimes the dragons, even Spark, had an infiniteness about them, an unknowableness that reminded Billy of what it felt like to look into the night sky. It made him feel very small and very fragile.

'Even those with good hearts have to make hard choices, Billy. And there is no point in looking back.'

'I just hope JJ is going to be okay,' said Billy.

'As do I,' said Spark. 'But right now you should be celebrating Dylan being back. You saved your friend, Billy. And, if you had to choose again, you would choose Dylan, would you not?' She gazed over her shoulder at him, and her eyes darkened for a moment.

'That isn't what happened! There wasn't a choice,'

said Billy. 'It isn't like we traded one for the other. JJ *wanted* to go in the tree.' Even though Billy didn't answer Spark's question out loud, he knew the answer. He would have always chosen Dylan. But, instead of making him feel better, it made him feel worse.

'Exactly as you say,' said Spark. 'He wanted to go in the tree. You cannot take responsibility for others' actions. Humans, and dragons, will do things you won't understand or won't like, but it isn't your fault.' She turned her head again to look him in the eye. 'JJ being in that tree isn't your fault. Old Gold taking Dylan isn't your fault. None of this is your fault. Do not blame yourself for the bad choices made by others. You are a light in both realms, Billy Chan. You will help fight the dark.'

It was an epic speech, even for a dragon, and Billy felt embarrassed by how much faith she had in him. He hoped he wouldn't let her down.

'Thanks, Spark,' he said finally. Then he looked ahead at his friends and towards the future they were working to save. Together.

*

When the dragons were certain they had flown far enough from the tree, far enough from where the Dragon of Death would be going, they searched for a place to sleep for the night. They all needed rest. Especially Dylan. He kept closing his eyes, and Billy was glad that the bond he had with Buttons would keep him from falling off. They flew in tighter formation now, scanning the skies for a safe haven.

'JJ will tell Old Gold and the Dragon of Death everything,' said Xing flatly. 'The Dragon of Death will be searching for us. She will want revenge on us for sending her back in time in the first place. For not joining her and the nox-wings. And she will know that we have four of the pearls she seeks. I do not think it is wise for us to sleep on the ground as we did last night, even with a protective enchantment.'

'What about a floating island?' Ling-Fei suggested, pointing at one above them. 'I don't think I sense anything living on that one. Perhaps we could sleep there?'

'A wise thought, my human,' said Xing. 'Let us go close to the one you see. If it is suitable, we will come back for the others.' She raced higher and higher into the sky, heading towards the floating island.

The other dragons hovered. Dylan's eyes drooped shut. 'I'm so tired,' he said. 'I've barely slept since Old Gold took me through that portal. Every time I fell asleep, I was sure he'd kill me or sacrifice me or leave me. I was constantly using my persuasion power on him to stay alive.'

'It wouldn't have worked on the Dragon of Death,' said Buttons.

Dylan shuddered. 'I can't imagine how terrible it would have been to be close to her. I'm not looking forward to facing her again, I'll tell you that much.' Then he scrunched his face up. 'I'm still feeling a bit sick, to be honest. But I've been feeling sick ever since I swallowed my pearl, so that might have something to do with that.'

'You did *what*?' said Charlotte.

'I knew Old Gold was desperate to have a pearl! You heard what he did to Ling-Fei's grandparents to get the Lightning Pearl.'

As if in response, the Lightning Pearl grew hot against the skin on Billy's chest.

'Swallowing it was the only way I could think of to keep it safe,' said Dylan. 'And my powers still worked too. One day I tested it by asking Old Gold to stop and make a fire, and he did!'

'Should we all swallow our pearls?' asked Billy.

'What is this inane chat about swallowing pearls?' said Xing, who had swooped in behind the group silently. 'Wait, tell me when we get to that island up there. It's empty. Come.'

The group flew to the small floating island. When they landed, Billy realized what probably should have been obvious – because the island wasn't tethered to anything, it drifted slowly. It felt a little bit like being on top of a giant hot-air balloon. He made sure to stay in the middle of it.

'Tell me what happened to your pearl!' Xing demanded. Dylan explained.

Xing let out a sharp laugh. 'What a foolish and yet inspired thing to do.' Then her voice sharpened. 'Though the rest of you absolutely should not swallow your pearls. To carry that much power on your body is one thing, but to have it inside you . . .' Her voice trailed off.

'Even a dragon would not be able to withstand it for long,' said Spark softly, gazing at the stars just starting to come out all around them.

Dylan groaned and slumped to the ground. 'I thought I was doing the best thing.'

'There, there,' said Buttons, tenderly patting Dylan on the head – as tenderly as he could with his long claws. 'It was the best thing in the situation. And you successfully kept the pearl from both Old Gold and the Dragon of Death. That is no small achievement.'

'Have you been getting headaches? Dizzy spells? Feeling as if you might collapse or fall over?' said Xing.

Dylan nodded. 'I thought maybe that was because we weren't resting or eating much.' He looked around at the island. 'Speaking of, what have you guys been eating?'

'We had some fish . . . yesterday?' said Charlotte. 'And peaches today. Just peaches. We were on the move all day. We didn't want to lose any time finding you.'

'Thanks, guys, I really mean it. I know . . . I know you didn't have to come after me.' He paused and his brow furrowed. 'Hey, how did you find me anyway?'

'We were always going to find you,' said Buttons. 'There was no other option.'

'But we had some help from an ... unexpected source,' said Ling-Fei with a smile.

'Oh!' said Billy, tugging Dylan's Claddagh ring off his finger. 'That reminds me! I've been meaning to give this back to you.' He held out the ring.

'My ring! I don't believe it!' He put his ring on and looked around. 'Where's my pig?'

'Your pig?' Billy said with a laugh. 'I was starting to think of it as *my* pig.'

Dylan shook his head, grinning. 'Oh, no. That is *my* pig. It was one of the things that kept me going over the past few days. It would zoom by and land on my shoulder. Kept me company. It took a bit of charm, but Old Gold never even noticed it.' His face grew serious again. 'I was starting to get desperate, and I wanted to make sure there was ... some sign of me. In case the worst happened. Something for someone to find. I never thought the pig would actually bring you the ring!'

'Well, it did,' said Charlotte. 'Where has that little butterball got to anyway?'

'It led us to the tree and then it flew off,' said Ling-Fei.

'I'm sure it will be back,' said Tank. 'It seems fond of you all.'

'I've got this for you too,' said Billy. 'I've been wearing it while you were away. Hope you don't mind.' He slid off the backpack and handed it to Dylan with a grin. 'There should be a couple of peaches in there too.'

Dylan's eyes lit up. 'My backpack! And peaches! What a win.' He reached into the backpack and pulled out a peach. As he did, a gold coin tumbled out. 'What's this?' he said, picking it up and inspecting it.

'Billy, we told you to put that somewhere safe,' chided Tank. 'Not in a backpack. It could fall out at any moment.'

'Sorry,' said Billy. 'I just didn't want to be carrying a coin with a soul in it directly on me.'

'A *what*?' said Dylan, throwing the coin back on the ground.

Billy picked it up and slipped it into one of the almost invisible pockets hidden in his suit. 'But I guess it isn't fair to ask Dylan to carry it around.'

He explained to Dylan about the coin, and how he had come to have it in his possession.

'I know you all probably have a million questions for me,' Dylan said. 'I want to find out what you've been doing too—'

'Looking for you, obviously,' Charlotte interrupted.

Dylan managed a smile. 'But I'm so tired. Can I rest first? And then we can talk about everything.' He sighed. 'I wish we could go home.'

His comment hung in the air.

Billy cleared his throat. 'Dylan, you know we've got to make sure we stop the Dragon of Death. This is our chance. And Spark says that the best way of doing that is by gathering the rest of the pearls, and then we will be strong enough to fight her.'

'I know that. I just don't feel strong enough to do much of anything right now,' admitted Dylan. His nose was running, and he wiped it with the back of his hand.

'Dylan,' said Ling-Fei with a gentle smile. 'You'll be okay. We can't do this without you. We need you.'

'And right now what Dylan needs is rest,' said Buttons, bustling around like a nurse. 'Here, I'll make you a fire. Oh! And I'll go and catch some fish too. And then I'll sing you a lullaby. How does that sound?'

'Almost as good as going home,' said Dylan with a small grin. Then he doubled over, clutching his stomach. After a moment, he straightened up. 'Sorry, sorry. I've been getting these pains all day.'

'It's the pearl,' said Spark. 'It isn't meant to be in a stomach.'

'On the bright side, you know it will be out soon enough,' said Charlotte, thumping him on the back. 'What goes in must come out!'

Dylan groaned again. 'I don't like thinking about that either.' Then he smiled. 'At least I'll be with you guys when it happens!'

'Oh, no,' said Billy. 'Friendship only goes so far. You can deal with getting your pearl out all by yourself.'

A Secret

It was a relief to be all together again.

And to know that while they slept, the dragons would be watching over them, keeping them safe.

And yet Billy still couldn't sleep. He stared up at the dancing stars in the sky and the three moons. They looked close enough to touch.

He knew the stars could be called down – he'd seen Dimitrius do it. And Spark too. But there was something . . . unnatural about it. The stars belonged in the sky.

He wondered if swallowing a star hurt. And then he wondered how Dimitrius had even known how to *do* that. And what it meant that Spark had done something a nox-wing had done. His mind kept on going and going, asking questions that he didn't have answers to. He felt as if he were on a mental treadmill, running and running but not getting anywhere. Now that they had found Dylan, all the thoughts he'd locked away in his mind were coming out. He rolled over, trying to settle, and saw a familiar shape on the edge of the floating island.

Spark was keeping watch. Careful not to wake the others, Billy tiptoed over to her.

You should be sleeping, Spark said through their bond without turning round. Billy should have known she'd have sensed him coming. *You need to rest.*

I'll sleep when you do, Billy responded.

He felt Spark's smile. *Come, sit with me. The view is spectacular. Even in the dark.*

Billy crept to the edge and sat with his feet dangling over. Spark was right. Far, far below them the ocean glistened and glowed in the night under the three moons. This would have scared him once, being so high. But now he flew with dragons.

Heights no longer scared him. Besides, he knew if he were to fall, Spark would catch him.

When we fly, it is hard to appreciate the view below, thought Spark. *It is nice to stop. To be quiet.*

Would you rather be alone right now? Billy suddenly worried he was intruding. *I can go back to the others.*

No, your company is always welcome. Do you know that I've never bonded with a human before? I am young, in dragon years, and fewer humans cross into our realms these days. We were warned it was not safe to go into the Human Realm. I never thought I would know the joy of a human heart bond. Thank you for this gift.

Billy tried to find the right words to let Spark know how much she meant, how he felt like the luckiest kid in the universe, the luckiest kid to have ever existed, to have Spark as his dragon.

I know, Spark thought gently. *I know.*

They sat in silence again, and, for a moment, Billy relaxed. He wanted to stay like this, at peace with his dragon, the whole world beneath them.

But a thought had been burrowing around

in his brain like an unwelcome worm. And it wouldn't go away.

What is it? thought Spark, sensing Billy's unease.

You know how we used your hoard as the portal?

Of course. I was there.

Why . . . why did it need to be something living to give you the power to do that? Isn't that like . . . taking life force?

Spark sighed loudly. Some frost blew out of her nose. She turned her neck so she was looking at Billy with her glowing gold eyes. Then she blinked and for a moment Billy thought he saw her eyes go black. She blinked again and they returned to gold.

A chill ran through Billy. It was as if she'd blown that frosty air right into his heart.

When I swallowed that first star, I didn't know what I was doing. I knew I had to protect you, and it was the only way.

There was a strange desperation snaking through Spark's inner voice that Billy had never heard before. It made him nervous. He trusted Spark completely, but this caught him by surprise. He tried to think warm thoughts so Spark couldn't sense how anxious he was.

And I wasn't prepared for the power that it would fill me with. It was like . . . nothing else.

More powerful than heart-bonding with a human?

Spark paused.

The power that comes with our bond is like the power of the ocean. Steady. The power that came from swallowing the star was like . . . lightning striking a tree. A flash, a thunderclap, a sudden blaze and then nothing. But I was left with a hunger for it.

That doesn't sound pleasant at all, Billy thought back.

I understood, for the first time, why so many dragons had turned Noxious. You see, that taste of dark magic made me yearn for more. And I fear it will start to turn me too.

'That isn't fair!' Billy's voice rang out unexpectedly. He had spoken out loud without realizing. He looked behind him. His friends and their dragons still lay sleeping.

You did it to save me, he thought furiously down their bond. *That is a good thing. That is the opposite of evil!*

Dark magic does not know good or evil, it only knows power. And I knew that the only way we would be able to travel back in time would be for me to swallow a star again. I relished the thought, when it should have left me repulsed. Because you are right, Billy. Destroying my living hoard to make the portal was taking life force. As was swallowing the star. Stars were living things once, you know.

Billy felt as if time were slowing down around them. He felt the heaviness of what Spark was confiding settle round him like a suffocating blanket. One terrible question kept ricocheting round his brain and he steeled himself to ask it. He had to know. *Are you a nox-wing now?*

Spark sighed again. *It is not that simple. We told you when you joined us that it was a battle between good and evil, and back then I thought it was that straightforward. Now I know it is not.* She gazed at him again. *Do you think I am evil, Billy?*

Billy shook his head vehemently. *Never. Never, never, never. You are my dragon. If you have been . . . poisoned by dark magic, I will help you. There has to be a way.*

Spark nuzzled him gently, and the heaviness around him lifted a bit.

Perhaps your heart is good enough for both of us, Billy. I am glad you have not lost your faith in me.

Never, he thought again.

I do not like hiding this from the others. As my human, you needed to be the first to know, but I should tell the others too. Then they can decide if they still want me to be part of this mission we are on together.

But you are good! Billy thought back emphatically. *Telling everyone wouldn't help, it would just make them anxious.* He looked Spark directly in the eyes. *You did what you had to do. I know you, Spark, you do not have a dark heart. And we need you. I need you.*

I am doing my best to fight this urge for dark magic. And, as you say, even though it was dark magic, it was for good.

Exactly! We wouldn't have found Dylan without it. Of course it was for good. I bet as soon as you did something good with that power, it . . . balanced out! You are definitely good. Billy's thoughts were coming fast down the bond, as if he could make it true just by thinking it over and over. *You are good. I know you are.*

I am glad that of all the humans in the universe, you

135

are my human. I will need your help more than ever now, Spark thought.

I won't let you down, Billy thought. And then, just to be extra clear, he whispered it out loud too.

'I won't let you down.'

Swimming With Legends

The secret that Spark had shared with Billy burrowed into him until it felt as if it were his secret too.

The next morning, he was determined to do whatever he could to help her. He knew that together they were stronger than the pull of dark magic. Spark had said his goodness would be enough for both of them. He had to believe that. And he'd pay more attention to her emotions through their bond so he knew how she was feeling and knew when she needed his support.

And yet Billy couldn't look his friends in the eye. He worried that if he did, they would instantly know he was hiding something. And not just any something – something big.

But, if any of them did notice, nobody said so. Not Ling-Fei, who was usually so perceptive. Nor Charlotte, who was nosy and had a keen sense for when someone wasn't telling her everything. Nor Dylan, who was so happy and relieved to be reunited with them all. He probably wouldn't have noticed if Billy's nose fell off, Billy thought with a smile.

Billy could almost believe he had dreamed it. The only indication Spark gave to acknowledge what had passed between them was a conspiratorial nod over breakfast. The weight of her secret, and of being the only one who could help her, hung heavy on his shoulders. But he nodded back and managed a smile. He'd be there for his dragon.

Breakfast was peaches again.

'What I wouldn't give for a biscuit with apple butter and a pile of grits,' said Charlotte.

Dylan frowned. 'What are *grits*? Sounds like a type of dirt.'

'Um, excuse you. Grits are delicious, creamy goodness. And my favourite thing for breakfast.'

'That does sound good,' said Ling-Fei. 'I hope I can try it one day.'

Billy thought with longing about the pancakes his mom made on weekends. Then he started thinking about all the other foods he missed. Like hamburgers from the diner his older brother Eddie loved. And his dad's special fried rice.

And then he wasn't thinking about food at all, but his family. He missed them so much and so strongly that his chest hurt. He reached out to Spark, needing a little bit of reassurance.

Spark whipped her head up and sharpened her gaze on him. *Billy, are you all right?*

She must have felt his homesickness.

I'm fine, Billy thought back. *I just . . . miss my mom and dad. And my brother.*

Spark's eyes softened. *Of course*, she thought. *You are a long way from home.*

Billy nodded and swallowed the lump in his throat. He didn't want to tell the others he was homesick. He didn't want them to think he was weak. And, more than that, he worried that if he started talking about how much he missed his family, it would remind them that they were far from their homes too. Dylan had already mentioned how much he couldn't wait to go back. If they all began to feel like this, they wouldn't be able to get anything done.

They didn't have time to be homesick.

They had a mission to complete.

Billy took a decisive bite of his peach and looked at his friends and their dragons. 'We need a plan,' he said.

'We have to find the other pearls before the Dragon of Death does,' said Ling-Fei, nibbling on her own peach. She glanced up at Xing. 'Right?'

'Yes,' said Xing. 'The more pearls the Dragon of Death has, the stronger she will be. She is already the strongest dragon we've ever encountered and she is gaining more strength every day. Look at the land. Remember how it was when we arrived? And now there are signs of dark magic throughout. I am sure you have all noticed even the sky is beginning to change, and those putrid purple plants are sprouting up everywhere.'

'Xing is right. The Dragon of Death is growing more and more powerful. If we have the pearls, we stand a much better chance of stopping the Dragon of Death for good,' said Tank in his low voice.

'There are many legends about the pearls and their

powers,' added Buttons. 'All we know for certain is that they can unlock and amplify power, as they have for you four. But no one knows what else the pearls can do.'

Spark was quiet. Billy knew that she was thinking about how she had used dark magic to increase her own power. Billy wondered if Xing, with her ability to sense magic, suspected Spark's secret. After all, they had all seen Spark swallow the star. But what they didn't know was the impact it was having on Spark. How it had made her crave more dark magic. If anyone else was going to be able to tell that Spark was having an internal battle, it would surely be Xing, Billy thought. But she seemed unaware, for now. Billy hoped it stayed that way.

'Ah, I see you guys haven't got any better at making plans while I've been gone,' said Dylan. 'Lots of bold statements but no details. It's a miracle you found me really.'

'The important thing is, we did find you,' said Billy with a grin. 'But you're right, we need to figure out what to do first.'

'All I can think about is how much I stink,'

moaned Charlotte. 'I haven't had a shower in . . .' She frowned, counting on her fingers. 'I'm losing track of time. But I do know I've *never* gone this long without showering.' She tried to run a hand through her hair. 'And my hair has definitely never been this tangled or this dirty.'

'You could cut it off,' suggested Xing with a sharp glint in her eyes. 'My claws are sharp enough.'

Charlotte gasped and stepped back. 'Absolutely not! Do you know how long it took me to grow it out?'

'I do not,' said Xing drolly. 'The speed of human hair growth is not something that has ever interested me.'

'Back to how much Charlotte stinks,' said Dylan.

'Hey!' said Charlotte, glowering at him.

'I was just going to say I bet you don't smell as bad as I do,' Dylan said quickly.

'For creatures with such an undeveloped sense of smell, you are complaining quite a lot about scent,' said Xing.

'Oh, be nice,' said Buttons. 'You forget that they are still hatchlings.' He stepped protectively next to Dylan.

'I have an idea,' said Billy. He glanced over the edge of the island and grinned. 'Who's up for a swim?'

The dragons insisted on finding shallow waters, where they could keep an eye out for any sea creatures that might fancy a human snack, and eventually they found a small cove.

Billy, Dylan, Ling-Fei and Charlotte peeled off their protective suits to their tank tops and underwear. After some cajoling from Charlotte, Tank hung their suits on his horns to keep them dry.

'I'm a dragon,' Billy heard him mutter. 'Not a clothes rack.' Billy knew Tank would do anything for Charlotte though, including looking undignified.

At first, Billy thought he might feel self-conscious, but once they were in the water he relaxed. It felt as if they were in swimsuits, swimming in the local pool.

Of course, the Forgotten Sea was much better than a swimming pool. The water was surprisingly warm. Because of the citrus smell that permeated the Forgotten Sea, dipping into it felt like taking a lemon-scented bath.

'This is *glorious*!' sang Charlotte as she came up from dunking her whole head under the water.

Billy had forgotten how much he missed the ocean. Any ocean. Even one that smelled like lemons and oranges. He floated on his back and looked up at the sky – at the islands floating overhead that now seemed normal, and at the three moons he had grown so used to.

'My nan is right,' said Dylan, doggy-paddling next to him. Remarkably, Dylan still had his glasses on. 'Cleanliness really is next to godliness.' Billy noticed something glinting around Dylan's neck.

'Hey! You've got your pearl back,' he said. 'Guessing the . . . retrieval went okay?'

'Gross,' said Charlotte, wrinkling her nose.

'Yep! What goes in must come out and all that. I'll admit that it was one of the reasons I was eager to take any kind of bath today,' said Dylan.

'I hope we don't hear the Screaming Serpent again,' said Ling-Fei as she swam round in a small circle. 'If we could feel the vibrations in the air, imagine how bad it would be in the sea itself!'

Tank shook his head, and the protective suits

hanging off his horn swung in the air. He was the only dragon not in the water and flew in slow circles above them, keeping watch. Buttons floated on his back, his large belly protruding out of the gentle waves of the Forgotten Sea. Xing swirled and undulated around them, and Spark floated on the surface of the water, paddling her legs beneath her like a swan.

'It is likely that we heard the Screaming Serpent's dying screams,' Tank said. 'If our theory about the Dragon of Death taking the Coral Pearl from her are correct, I doubt she would have left the Screaming Serpent alive. And she will now be searching for the rest of the pearls. That leaves the Ice Pearl and the Diamond Pearl. We must find them before she does. We need to make sure she never has the Eight Great Treasures all together.'

'Those pearls could be anywhere!' said Charlotte, kicking with frustration in the water.

Something occurred to Billy. 'If the Dragon of Death is trying to get all eight pearls, and we have four of them, doesn't it make more sense for us to go back to our own time and bring the pearls with us? That way the Dragon of Death will never have all eight.' He was proud of himself for figuring this out.

'I wish it were that simple,' said Buttons. 'As we've told you, there is much about the magic of the pearls that even we dragons do not know or understand. But we do know from dragon legend that there can only ever be eight pearls in one time but there must always be all eight pearls.'

Billy frowned. 'That sounds like a riddle.'

'If we go back to our time with the four pearls, that does not mean they will disappear for ever in this time,' Buttons went on. 'Four more will replace them. And where they will appear we do not know. The best way to keep the pearls from the Dragon of Death is to find the remaining ones, the Ice Pearl and the Diamond Pearl, and then defeat her once and for all. Only then can we go back to our time, bringing our pearls with us, safe in the knowledge that when the pearls appear again in this time, the Dragon of Death will not be around to find them.'

'So what happened to the Lightning Pearl in this

time before we arrived?' said Billy, clutching his pearl to his chest. It fizzed with a familiar heat. 'How come mine didn't disappear?'

'You are a dragon-bonded human. There is great power in that. It is most likely that the Lightning Pearl in this time did not have anything to be grounded to, and simply disappeared,' explained Tank.

'This makes my head hurt,' said Dylan.

'It makes sense to me,' said Ling-Fei softly. 'Our pearls have magic in them, and magic acts like a living thing.'

'I wonder . . .' said Xing. 'The Coral Pearl was deep in the Forgotten Sea, hoarded by the Screaming Serpent, just as legend says. One of the other pearls we are looking for, the Ice Pearl, has a legend about it too . . .' Her voice trailed off.

Everyone stared at Xing and waited for her to go on. She stared back.

'Oh, come on!' Charlotte burst out. 'This is not the time for suspenseful statements! Although I do appreciate a good dramatic pause.'

'As I was saying,' Xing sniffed, 'legend has it that the Ice Pearl is hidden deep in—'

'The Frozen Wasteland!' Buttons burst out. 'Of course! I should have figured it out.'

'Wow, Buttons, you really stole Xing's moment there,' said Dylan.

Xing growled.

'Excuse my interruption,' said Buttons. 'I just got excited.'

'Back to the Ice Pearl,' said Billy. 'What is the Frozen Wasteland?' It didn't sound like a place he wanted to go.

Tank looked at Spark. 'Spark, do you want to tell them?'

Spark nodded and flung a wing up, sending a wall of water flying into the air. It froze instantly and pictures began to form on it.

'Long ago, before even this time, at the moment when dragons were new to the world, they had one common enemy.' Spark paused.

Billy waited in anticipation. What could be the great dragon enemy? Something epic, he was sure of it.

'Worms,' Spark said with a shudder.

'Worms?' spluttered Billy. 'Like ... earthworms?

Wriggly squishy things that come out when it rains? Birds eat them for breakfast?'

'I do not think we are talking about the same kind of worms,' Buttons said haughtily. 'Show them, Spark.'

On the ice wall a picture of a giant worm appeared. It was bigger than the dragons next to it, dwarfing them. It had big cloudy eyes and a huge gaping mouth.

'I mean, it does look pretty gross,' said Charlotte.

'I won't disagree with you,' said Xing. 'Disgusting, deadly things.'

'The legend goes that eventually the dragons forced the worms back into a cold, barren part of the realm,' Spark said. 'The Frozen Wasteland. And an enchantment was set, trapping the worms within, but also locking the dragons out. The worms and dragons could live as they pleased, never crossing paths.'

'Of course the worms got the worse end of the bargain,' said Tank. 'The Frozen Wastelands are aptly named.'

'But the worms are highly adaptable,' said Spark. 'I imagine they are flourishing. And for many it will be the only home they have known.'

'This has been an interesting lesson in dragon history and lore, but my fingers are getting all wrinkled from being in the sea for so long. Could we skip ahead to the part that involves the pearl?' said Dylan.

'The worms have it, don't they?' said Billy. *Of course* it wasn't going to be simple finding the Ice Pearl. Would they even be able to retrieve it? It sounded as if nobody who entered the Frozen Wasteland came out of it alive. It felt as if everything was stacked against them.

'We do not know for sure,' said Spark as the ice wall behind her sank back into the sea, dissolving. 'After all, no dragons have been there. But there is no whisper of it anywhere else in our realm, only in the Frozen Wasteland. It is possible the worms took it there with them. And there it stays.'

'How are we meant to get to the Frozen Wasteland if dragons can't get in?' said Billy, already starting to dread the answer.

'Well, you see, that is where things get a bit tricky,' said Buttons.

'I am moderately alarmed by the implication that

'things up to now haven't been tricky,' said Dylan.

'You four can probably get in,' said Tank. 'As far as I know, there is nothing stopping humans from entering the Frozen Wasteland.'

'But we can't go with you,' said Spark. 'You will have one another, and your pearl powers, and that will have to be enough.'

'We won't be able to help you if you need it,' said Xing. 'Or prepare you for what you might find.'

'On the bright side, you won't have to worry about running into the Dragon of Death,' added Buttons.

'She has Old Gold with her now. And JJ. What if they are planning the same thing?' said Ling-Fei.

'Ling-Fei is right,' said Xing. 'We must move quickly. Come, get out of the sea and dressed.'

'How are we meant to get there if you can't enter?' said Billy. Despite the warm water, he shivered.

'We must take you to the Blood Strait.'

The Blood Strait

'The Blood Strait?' said Dylan. 'That sounds horrible.'

They were back in their protective suits, astride their dragons. Preparing to go to the Blood Strait.

Billy didn't say anything out loud, but he agreed with Dylan. Everything about this plan, separating from the dragons and going into unknown territory, sounded terrible. He knew it was the only way, but he wasn't happy about it.

'The Blood Strait starts on our land and connects the Forgotten Sea to the Frozen Wasteland,' said Tank. 'While you are searching for the Ice Pearl, we will go after the Diamond Pearl. If we have six of the eight pearls, we should be strong enough to take on the Dragon of Death.'

'How will we find you again?' said Billy, trying to keep the panic out of his voice. It wasn't just being away from the dragons' protection that made him nervous. He didn't want to leave Spark when she was so vulnerable to the draw of dark magic. He'd promised he would help her. How could he do that if they were separated?

'Do not doubt the strength of our bonds,' said Spark. 'It will guide us to you and you to us. As it has done before.'

They flew back over the land, keeping watch for any signs of the Dragon of Death. Sure enough, more slain dragons dotted the landscape, their gold blood pooling beneath them, and purple plants growing around. Each dead dragon added more urgency to their mission, and they flew on even faster. Eventually, they came to the banks of a blood-red river.

The Blood Strait.

'Is it actually blood?' said Dylan, looking horrified as they landed near it. The red river bubbled and frothed and looked distinctly uninviting. Further along, it picked up speed, the rapids smashing against the riverbanks.

'It is not dragon blood,' said Xing loftily. 'You know we bleed gold. It smells and tastes of the blood of lesser creatures, such as yourselves.'

'It feels ... alive,' said Ling-Fei, edging closer.

'And so it is,' said Tank. 'It is one of the veins of this land. And it is forbidden for dragons to enter it.'

'This is as far as we can take you,' said Buttons.

'Are we meant to *swim* in it?' demanded Charlotte. 'Billy's a pretty good swimmer, but I bet even he couldn't manage that. And there is no way the rest of us could. Do you see how fast that current is? And something tells me that even with our suits on we wouldn't want to come in direct contact with that.' She wrinkled her nose in distaste.

'Your instincts are right. The blood is thick and unpleasant to be in. And, more importantly, you would be unable to hold your breath for as long as you need to when it goes beneath the ice into the Frozen Wasteland,' said Spark. 'There is another way.' She paused and gazed into the distance.

'Surely the smell of the humans will have attracted it by now,' said Xing.

'Attracted what?' said Billy, immediately on guard.

'Our dragon scent could be masking the human smell,' said Buttons. He looked at Dylan apologetically. 'We're going to have to leave you sooner than we would have liked. But together you will be okay.'

The Blood Strait began to bubble and churn suddenly. An enormous fish rose out of the water, its head landing with a thud on the land, its body and tail remaining submerged. Its tail thrashed back and forth, splashing blood everywhere. Billy jumped back, but he wasn't fast enough. A splatter of blood sprayed across his face.

'Ew,' said Charlotte, taking a step away.

The fish was an iridescent white, with two large horns protruding from its head and sharp spines jutting out of its back. It stared at them with huge white eyes on either side of its head.

'The stench of dragons offends me,' gargled the fish in a voice like the harsh crash of water on stone. Billy could see rows and rows of jagged red teeth.

'But beneath that foul smell is the sweet scent of *humans*. And my eyes confirm it. How rare. How delicious.' It stuck out a fat white tongue and licked its own eyeball. 'A treat for the nose, the eyes and the tongue.'

'I would like to go back to the tree, please,' said Dylan, stepping closer to Buttons.

'Tell me, dragons, what brings you to the Blood Strait?' the fish asked. 'This is not your domain. A step further and . . .'

'Yes, yes, if we enter the strait or go near the Frozen Wasteland, our scales will sizzle until we are no more,' snapped Xing. 'We know the legend.'

'Not a mere legend, but the truth,' gargled the fish. 'You must have a good reason for coming this close.' Its eyes rolled around, taking them in, before zeroing in on Billy. Billy swallowed hard but made himself stare straight back. He wasn't going to be intimidated by a fish. 'And for bringing such tasty morsels with you.'

'We come seeking a favour,' said Buttons, sounding pained. 'You can go where we cannot. And where our humans have need to be.'

'Your penchant for bargaining is well known,' said Spark. 'Perhaps we can come to an understanding.'

'I do no business with dragons,' the fish said. 'I chose my side long ago. Begone, foul flying beasts. Leave me with your hatchling humans.'

'If you harm them,' hissed Xing, 'know that we will seek retribution.'

Billy felt strangely comforted by her protective threat. They were going into dangerous and uncharted territory, and it was nice to know that, even from afar, their dragons would still be looking out for them. He personally would not want to be on the wrong side of Xing's wrath and hoped the fish felt the same.

'I will do as I wish. Now, begone or there will be no bargain.'

Still the dragons paused.

Are you sure this is the only way to the Frozen Wasteland? Billy thought to Spark.

I wish we knew another way, she thought back. *Use your wits, stay together. You will survive, and you will succeed.*

As always, Spark's belief in him made Billy feel

better. He stood a little straighter and looked at his friends and the rest of the dragons.

'We can do this,' he said, trying to sound confident. 'We'll find you after.'

'Billy's right,' said Charlotte. 'We'll be fine.' She looked the fish in the eye. 'I'm not scared of a *fish*,' she said scathingly.

The fish's tongue flicked out in response, but Charlotte just glared.

'And we'll be together,' added Ling-Fei, moving closer to Charlotte and Billy.

'I'd forgotten how I'm never consulted about anything,' grumbled Dylan, but he stepped towards the Blood Strait anyway.

'Now we must leave you,' thundered Tank. 'Do not lose faith in yourselves or one another.'

Be strong, Billy. You can do this. Spark's gold eyes focused on Billy. He hoped she was right. And he hoped she would be strong enough on her own to resist the pull of dark magic. He hated that they had to be separated.

As one, the four dragons rose into the air and flew away.

Billy, Ling-Fei, Charlotte and Dylan faced the giant fish alone.

'Tell me what it is you need,' said the fish. 'And then we'll discuss what I want from you.'

'We need to get to the Frozen Wasteland,' said Charlotte.

'Specifically to the Ice Pearl,' added Billy. 'If you know where that is.'

'You're in luck, as I know roughly where it was last seen,' said the fish. 'And I can take you there.'

Billy grinned at his friends.

'But not for free, of course,' the fish went on.

Before he realized he was doing it, Billy pressed his tongue to the gap between his teeth. The last time he'd done a trade with a strange creature, he'd ended up with two fewer teeth. He was wary of what the fish might want.

The fish licked its eyeball again. 'I'm going to have to eat one of you.'

The Life Price

Billy was sure he must have misheard the giant fish. But it kept talking.

'I'll let you decide amongst yourselves which one of you I eat.'

'Absolutely not,' said Billy. 'No deal.' They hadn't survived all this time in the Dragon Realm only for one of them to be sacrificed to a fish, of all things.

'Then no trip to the Frozen Wasteland,' said the fish, sounding bored. 'I need a life payment to swim through the Blood Strait. There is no other way.'

The friends looked at one another. 'What kind of life?' asked Charlotte slowly. 'Any life? Would a snail do? Surely we can find a snail around here.'

'Charlotte!' Ling-Fei said. 'All lives are worthy!'

'What? I would rather it be a snail than one of us!'

'A life heavy enough to sit in my belly,' said the fish. The word 'heavy' made Billy think of something.

'Wait a minute!' he said. He reached into the secret pocket in his suit and pulled something out. 'Would this do?' He held out the scratched gold soul coin. The eye shimmered and stared at him. Billy shuddered.

The fish blinked.

'It's a soul coin,' said Billy.

'I've never tasted a soul coin,' gurgled the fish, eyeing it.

'I think a soul coin should be worth a return trip,' said Dylan suddenly. 'For all four of us. Safe passage there and back. Gold *and* a soul? What a prize.'

'I will accept the soul coin to take you across the Blood Strait.'

'And back,' said Dylan meaningfully. He looked at the others. 'We don't want to get stranded somewhere called the Frozen Wasteland.'

'The bargain is done,' said the fish. It opened its gaping mouth further, its lower jaw dropping like a drawbridge. Its thick white tongue flopped out.

Billy hesitantly placed the gold coin in its mouth. The fish swallowed loudly. Then it stuck its tongue out again and licked its lips.

'Delicious,' it said.

'So, do we sit on your back?' said Billy.

'To reach the Frozen Wasteland, you take the Blood Strait and go beneath the ice,' said the fish. 'You would not survive on my back. You must ride in my mouth.'

'I don't think we'll survive in your mouth either!' said Charlotte.

'You have paid the life price. I will not eat you. As delicious as I'm sure you all would be.'

'I think it's telling the truth,' said Ling-Fei. 'It isn't going to eat us.'

'Well, in that case, I think we should . . . trust the fish,' said Billy. He couldn't believe this was actually something he was saying out loud, but he knew it was the only way to get to the Frozen Wasteland. This was their one chance of finding the Ice Pearl and ultimately stopping the Dragon of Death.

Charlotte took the first hesitant step forward, then she leaned back and looked directly in the fish's giant eye. 'You'd better not try anything . . . fishy,' she said. 'Otherwise I'll tear you apart from the inside.'

The fish blinked. 'I do not see how that would help you, as then you would be stuck inside a dead fish in the Blood Strait.'

'All I'm saying is that I always go down swinging,' said Charlotte, shaking her fist.

'Charlotte,' said Billy, behind her. 'Please just get inside the fish.'

'What a sentence,' said Dylan, shaking his head. 'But, ah, remember, fish, we do have a bargain. The soul coin has bought us a safe round-trip passage.'

The fish's eyes widened. 'There is no guarantee of safety. Something bigger than me could eat me. We could be stuck under the ice for ever. A lightning bolt could fry me.' The fish had no shoulders, but Billy could have sworn it shrugged. 'There is much danger and very little safety.'

'As is the way with everything here. We really should be used to this by now,' muttered Dylan.

Ling-Fei leaned forward and put her hand on the fish's cheek. 'I think what my friend means is as-safe-as-possible passage, right, Dylan?'

'Right,' said Dylan, who was looking paler by the minute.

'Well, let's stop wasting time talking about it and get going,' said Billy. He took a deep breath and stepped into the fish's mouth.

It was dark and wet inside the fish's mouth. And it smelled terrible.

'We are putting a lot of trust in a giant fish that expects payment in *lives* not to swallow us whole,' muttered Dylan as they all crowded in.

'I don't think we had much choice,' said Billy.

'I trust the fish,' Ling-Fei announced. 'I don't think it is going to do us harm. I'm pretty sure the soul coin bound it to its word.'

'All the same, I'm going to be channelling all the charm I've got into convincing it not to eat us,' said Dylan under his breath.

'Are you ready?' the fish said, its giant tongue waggling beneath them. 'This is the last time I'll speak to you. I need to keep my mouth closed on the journey, for obvious reasons.'

Dylan put his hand to the Granite Pearl around

his neck. 'We're ready, and we trust that you are going to carry us safely to the Frozen Wasteland and as close to the Ice Pearl as you can get us.'

It was impossible to know if Dylan's power would work on the fish. But Billy figured it couldn't hurt. He was so glad Dylan was with them again. And it wasn't just because of his power of persuasion. Being with Dylan both cheered Billy and made him feel more confident about facing whatever lay ahead.

'Let's sit closer together,' Ling-Fei suggested. 'It's going to be dark when the fish shuts its mouth.'

'Good idea,' said Billy.

'Be careful not to stab yourself on one of its teeth,' said Charlotte, eyeing the sharp red teeth around them, each one the size of a sword.

'Are we going to be able to breathe?' said Dylan, taking in a big gulp of air.

Ling-Fei's face grew serious for a moment as she focused. 'Yes,' she said. 'I can sense that there will be enough air in here for us for a while. Not for ever, but hopefully enough for the journey there.'

'That is . . . moderately reassuring,' said Dylan.

'We'll be fine,' said Billy with more confidence than he felt.

They arranged themselves in a tight circle. Billy positioned himself closest to the back of the fish's mouth; he figured, with his power of agility, he could keep the others from slipping down the fish's throat and could clamber out if he fell in.

'Hold on tight,' said the fish, and then it closed its jaws.

Now it was very, *very* dark.

There was a sudden lurch and Billy realized the fish must have been diving down into the Blood Strait. The four friends tumbled forward in a tangle of arms and legs, knocking against the fish's tightly clenched teeth. Billy heard the sound of the Blood Strait rushing by and braced himself, preparing for it to come pouring in, for them to not only drown but drown inside the mouth of a giant fish. But the fish's mouth remained sealed shut and the fish dived down and down.

'Is everyone okay?' Billy said.

'I will be when you move your knee out of my side,' huffed Charlotte.

'My ears are popping,' Dylan said with a groan.

'We're going very deep,' said Ling-Fei. Her pearl power gave her awareness of their surroundings. She pursed her lips, concentrating. 'I think we're underneath land now. Or maybe ice.'

Billy tried not to let that add to the feeling of claustrophobia that was creeping in on him. He had gone ice skating once with his older brother on a frozen lake in the mountains. He'd enjoyed it until he'd accidentally strayed onto thin ice in the middle of the lake and fallen through. It'd been so cold he'd gone numb almost instantly. His skates had dragged him down quickly and, in his panic, he'd swum in the wrong direction, bumping his head on the ice above. He'd forced himself to calm down and swim back to where he'd fallen in, where Eddie was half submerged himself, arms in the water, reaching for Billy. His brother had pulled him up and out, and they had dragged themselves back to solid land where they'd collapsed in a soggy heap.

He'd managed to calm himself then, so he could do it now. Billy forced himself to breathe slowly and steadily. They weren't trapped. They were fine. He was fine. Or as fine as someone could be while in the mouth of a giant fish.

After what felt like ages of being cramped on top of one another in the dark, feeling as if they were in the nose of a diving plane, the fish levelled out. Billy waited to make sure they really were level and then crawled to the middle of the fish's mouth. He reached inside the collar of his protective suit and pulled out the Lightning Pearl.

The storm inside it was raging, tiny lightning bolts flashing. It only gave off a faint pulsing blue light, but it meant they weren't in complete darkness.

'Good idea,' said Ling-Fei, taking her pearl out too. The Jade Pearl's green glow joined the blue hue. Charlotte and Dylan followed suit, with the Gold Pearl and the Granite Pearl. Together the combined light cast an eerie glow on their faces in the darkness.

'I remember when I thought sitting in a cave that walked would be the strangest mode of travel I'd ever take,' said Dylan, pushing his glasses up his nose.

'Those glasses are indestructible,' said Charlotte.

Dylan took them off and studied them. 'You

know, now that you mention it, I think Xing must have cast an enchantment of some kind on them when the dragons gave us our suits. She must like me more than she lets on.'

There was a low rumble from deep inside the fish's stomach. The friends scooted closer together.

'We'll have to be careful when it resurfaces,' said Billy, looking over his shoulder towards the fish's throat. 'We don't want to end up in its belly.'

'What's our plan when we get to the Frozen Wasteland?' said Charlotte.

'*If* we get to the Frozen Wasteland, you mean,' said Dylan.

'We have to stay positive,' said Ling-Fei.

'Ling-Fei,' said Billy, 'do you think you'll be able to sense the Ice Pearl?'

'It depends how close we are,' said Ling-Fei. 'I'll try my best.'

'Yet again we have no plan, but we aren't letting that stop us from leaping straight into danger,' said Dylan.

'I'd say it is more like diving into danger,' said Charlotte with a smirk.

'We totally have a plan,' said Billy. 'We get in, we get the pearl, we get out. It is basically foolproof.'

'Fool being the key word in that sentence,' said Dylan, but he was grinning. 'It's good to be back with you lot again. Even if we are in a giant fish's mouth, heading towards certain doom. Nobody else I'd rather be with, to be honest.'

'Well, that's good, because you're stuck with us,' said Charlotte.

Billy knew what Dylan meant. He felt the same way. Being together, even without the dragons, filled him with a sense of calm strength.

As the giant fish swam through the depths, Billy wondered what they would find when they arrived at the Frozen Wasteland. Nobody mentioned the possibility that Old Gold or even JJ might have reached the Ice Pearl first.

Or that they might not make it back to their dragons.

Just when Billy thought he might be sick from the smell of fish insides and the lack of fresh air, Ling-Fei lifted her head, suddenly alert.

'Something is happening,' she said. 'I think we're close.'

Billy tensed and pressed himself hard against the side of the mouth so he wouldn't fall back into its belly. A moment later, the fish lurched forward and landed with a hard flop, sending them all tumbling.

'We must be here,' said Billy. Nerves and excitement buzzed through him. He didn't know what to expect.

The fish opened its mouth and white, bright light and cold air rushed in to greet them.

'Welcome to the Frozen Wasteland. I have brought you as close to the Ice Pearl as I can,' said the fish. 'Now get out.'

'How will we find you later?' said Billy, squinting in the brightness. 'Do we come back here?'

'You have until sunset. I won't wait any longer. If you aren't back by then, it is almost certainly because you're all dead.'

The Frozen Wasteland

'Dead?' spluttered Dylan. 'What if we're just running a little late?'

'Even I do not dare to stay here after the sun goes down. The drifters grow too hungry. I do not wish to be caught in their tentacles.'

'The drifters?' said Ling-Fei, peering out. The icy wind was biting, even from the relative safety of the fish's mouth.

'You'll soon find out,' said the fish. 'They are dangerous by day, and deadly by night. When the sun goes down, your human essence will be irresistible to them.'

'Well, we'll be out of here by then,' said Charlotte.

Billy could tell her confidence was a little forced.

'Unless the worms catch you. They can't see, but they know where you are. They'll swallow you whole or turn you to stone with their bite,' the fish went on.

There was a screech far off in the distance. Billy shuddered. 'Can't you tell us anything helpful?' he said.

'I've warned you enough as it is. But I'm in a generous mood so I'll offer one tip more. If you are unlucky enough to get bitten, the only thing that will save you is the breath of the Ember Flower that grows deep beneath the earth. Impossible for you to reach.'

'So no actual advice then,' muttered Dylan.

'You are wasting valuable time. The sun will set sooner than you think. If I do not see you again, do not worry. I will tell others of the tale of four small humans who thought they could defeat the Wasteland Worm. It will bring amusement to many. Now go.'

'But . . .'

'I SAID GO!' bellowed the fish, and without

warning it spat them out onto the unforgiving, icy shores of the Frozen Wasteland.

By the time Billy had got to his feet, the only sign the fish had ever been there was a splatter of blood on the ice and a few bubbles in the Blood Strait. He looked around and realized they would have to scramble up an icy bank to get their bearings. He took a deep breath and instantly regretted it. The air was so cold it burned his throat and his lungs. 'At least that pool of blood can be how we mark this spot,' he said, 'so we know where to meet the fish after we find the Ice Pearl.'

'Do you really think the giant fish will be waiting for us?' said Charlotte, shivering.

'I think it has to,' said Ling-Fei softly. 'That gold soul coin bound it to its word.'

'But only until the sun sets,' said Dylan, coughing a little in the cold. 'Pretty rubbish deal, if you ask me.'

'A bargain is a bargain,' said Ling-Fei. 'The fish set the terms, but it won't break them.' She looked up at the white sky. 'The cold is making it hard to focus, but I'll try to sense the Ice Pearl so at least we know which direction to go in.'

The wind whipped round them, cutting through their protective suits. The suits had not been made to withstand the cold of the Frozen Wasteland.

Spark, Billy thought. *Can you hear me? I don't know if we can do this.*

Silence and cold was the only response. Billy closed his eyes and hunched his shoulders against the stinging chill. And then a small burst of heat, no bigger than a candle flame, rushed through him, enough to warm him just a little. It had to have been Spark sending hope, sending warmth, through their bond.

It was the motivation Billy needed. He rolled his shoulders back and faced his friends.

'Ling-Fei, I believe in you. You can sense the pearl. I believe in all of us. The dragons do too,' he said. He hoped they didn't notice his teeth chattering in the cold. 'We can do this. We *have* to do this.'

Another gust of wind flew at them so strongly it threatened to send them crashing into the Blood Strait. Ling-Fei stumbled and Charlotte grabbed her arm, pulling her up the bank. It was slippery, but Charlotte dug her heels in, securing them both.

'Let's move away from here,' said Charlotte, eyeing the Blood Strait uneasily. 'I don't want to freeze to death, but I don't like the idea of falling into a river of sticky, probably poisonous blood either.'

They moved slowly further up the bank of the strait, heads down, pushing against the wind. Billy's feet scrambled for purchase on the icy ground. Then they were on the plateau and the Frozen Wasteland opened out in front of them.

Billy stared at the wide expanse. The land looked like a thrashing ocean that had frozen in place at the height of a hurricane. Everywhere he looked, rock formations rose out of the ground like huge curling waves. Wind howled across the land, kicking up billows of ice and frost that swirled through the air like tornadoes. Strange, glowing, cloud-like blobs floated above in a dark grey sky.

Billy felt as if he had stepped into a horror movie, and for a brief moment he wondered whether they might have been better off staying in the fish and going back to their dragons empty-handed. How could they possibly navigate this strange land, let alone locate a pearl that could be hidden anywhere?

It seemed hopeless. He pushed the thought out of his mind. He had to stay positive.

'Talk about finding a needle in a haystack,' said Dylan, echoing Billy's thoughts. He clutched his arms across his chest for warmth as he scanned the horizon. 'Even if we knew which direction to go in, how are we going to find a tiny Ice Pearl in a place that is already *covered* in ice?'

'Well, we're never going to find it with that attitude,' said Charlotte. 'Ling-Fei, do you have any sense of where the pearl might be?'

Ling-Fei closed her eyes and touched the tips of her fingers to her temples.

The group watched expectantly. Billy could see his friend's eyes darting back and forth under her eyelids. He hoped this would work. After a few moments, Ling-Fei shook her head and opened her eyes. 'This place has an odd energy to it. I can't explain it, but it feels . . . unnatural somehow. It's making it hard for me to sense the pearl. But I can feel magic, which I guess could be from the pearl in this direction.' She pointed into the wasteland.

Billy followed Ling-Fei's outstretched hand and

tried to make out a distinguishable landmark to set their path. All he could see were rows and rows of the wave-like rock formations that blended together as seamlessly as the waves of an ocean. He couldn't help feeling that they were heading into an endless void. But he trusted Ling-Fei. And they didn't have anything else to go on. Together they were strong. 'Lead the way, Ling-Fei.'

The four children slowly pushed their way into the Frozen Wasteland, following Ling-Fei's senses. As they went deeper, Billy noticed something he wished he hadn't. There weren't just rocks and ice covering the wasteland, but thousands upon thousands of bones. He hadn't realized until he heard a distinct crack under his foot and looked down to see that he'd stepped on the skull of some unknown creature, the white of its bone blending in with the white of the snow and ice. Billy focused his eyes on the ground around him and found that everywhere he looked were the remains of strange creatures. He wondered how long these skeletons had been scattered here and hoped for their sakes that it was a long, long time – and whatever it was that had separated life from bone was long gone.

Billy looked up to see that Dylan had come to the same conclusion.

'Um, guys, do you see all these skeletons stuck in the snow?' he said.

Ling-Fei nodded solemnly. 'Poor creatures. This is a terrible, terrible place.' She paused and closed her eyes again. 'I think the pearl is close, but I can't tell which direction any more.'

'You're doing great,' said Charlotte. 'We would never have gotten this far without you.' She glanced at Billy. 'Maybe you can climb on one of these rocks and see if you can spot anything . . . other than rocks?'

Billy examined the rock formation closest to their group. Like all the other rock formations, this one curved out of the ground like a shark fin. Jagged icicles clung to the underside of the curve, almost like teeth. Climbing wouldn't be a problem, especially with his pearl power. Billy took two quick steps forward and leaped halfway up the rock, latching onto the sheer rock face like a spider and effortlessly climbing the rest of the way up. He glanced back at his friends with a smile. No matter how many times he used his power, it still felt good.

'Okay, okay,' said Dylan. 'We get it. You're really good at climbing. Now tell us what you see!'

Billy cupped his hands round his face as gusts of wind flung little bits of ice in all directions. The wind was much stronger at the top of the rock. He squinted into the distance, trying to see what was up ahead, but all he could make out were the few rock formations in front of them and, beyond that, a flurry of white and grey. Billy sighed and looked harder, trying to find some sort of clue. As he did, he realized that the flurry of white and grey wasn't the snow and ice in the air, but in fact an enormous circular clearing a short distance away.

'Tell us what you see,' shouted Charlotte from down below.

'One second,' Billy replied. 'I'm looking!'

'It's FREEZING down here!' Charlotte shouted back. 'So look faster!'

'It's pretty cold up here too!' Billy yelled. And then he looked down and what he saw made his blood freeze. Behind his friends crept a giant scorpion.

A thick, muscular tail curled high above its body, its long, sharp stinger aimed directly at Dylan. Its pincers opened and closed menacingly.

'Dylan!' cried Billy. 'Behind you!'

Dylan turned and fell when he saw the scorpion, landing hard on his back. The scorpion jolted forward, closing the distance between them as it raised its tail, ready to attack. Dylan scurried backwards, but Billy could see that he wasn't going to be fast enough to get away.

He had to save Dylan – he couldn't let his friend down again. He felt a burst of adrenaline and his instincts took over as he ran towards the edge of the rock. Everything around him seemed to move in slow motion, and, by the time he'd reached the edge of the rock, the scorpion had hardly moved at all. He dived off the rock towards the creature, crashing into its tail just as its long stinger was about to strike Dylan, then landed gracefully beside his friend as the stinger struck the earth next to them.

The creature hissed and swung an open pincer at Billy, who dodged the attack easily. Before the scorpion could make another move, Billy hopped onto its head and jammed his fingers into one of its beady black eyes. The scorpion hissed again and tried to swipe Billy off, but its claws couldn't reach him. Billy could sense its desperation as it swung its stinger down to strike him. At the last moment, Billy jumped out of the way, grabbed the stinger and thrust the sharp point into the scorpion's head. It twitched a few times before it stilled.

'I see you used my signature poke-the-giant-monster-in-the-eyeball move,' said Charlotte.

Billy smiled. 'Works every time.' He didn't tell the others how much his heart was racing or that his palms were sweating. His pearl power had taken over in the moment, and he'd known exactly what to do. It had felt as natural as breathing, but now, as the adrenaline began to fade, he was aware how close they had been to getting killed. And that couldn't be the only dangerous thing around here. Who knew what other creatures were lurking in this strange new realm? He had to stay calm though – it was the only way to survive.

'That was terrifying!' said Dylan, running over to Billy. 'Are you okay?'

'Of course,' said Billy, wanting to be brave for his friends. 'Are *you* okay?'

Dylan grabbed Billy with both arms and squeezed him tight. 'You saved me. Thank you.'

'I know you would have done the same thing,' said Billy, returning the hug.

'You moved like lightning,' said Dylan, taking a step back. 'One moment I was definitely going to be a scorpion skewer and the next thing I know you're next to me and the scorpion somehow missed me!'

'You were awesome!' added Charlotte. 'I've never seen anything move so fast. You were practically a blur.'

'I can't explain it,' Billy said. 'It felt like my power levelled up. Something was triggered inside me, and my instincts took control.' He cleared his throat. 'I think it has to do with how long we've had the pearls, like our powers are growing the longer we wear them. And I knew I couldn't let you down again.'

Dylan pulled Billy in for another hug then cleared his throat too and took a step back. 'Now . . . to the task at hand,' said Dylan, walking slowly over to the scorpion and poking it tentatively. 'Definitely dead.'

Ling-Fei approached the scorpion and put a hand on its body. 'Dear scorpion, I'm sorry things had to end this way. I hope you rest well.'

'I'm not sorry,' said Charlotte.

'Me neither, to be honest. If it was going to be that scorpion or me, I'm glad it was the scorpion,' said Dylan.

'Just because I'm being respectful doesn't mean I wish it had stabbed you with its tail,' said Ling-Fei. 'Of course I'm glad you are alive.'

'Now that we've mourned the death of the giant scorpion that tried to kill us, can we get back to trying to find the pearl? The sun isn't getting any higher in the sky,' said Charlotte.

'Yes, Billy, did you see anything while you were up there?' said Ling-Fei. 'We're definitely close – I can sense it.'

'There's a clearing on the far side of these rocks that I think we should check out. There might be something there.'

'Something like ... more ice?' said Dylan.

'Do you have any better ideas?' said Billy with a grin.

'You know my skill set is critiquing the plans, not coming up with them,' said Dylan, grinning back. 'Onwards!'

Hidden In Plain Sight

Billy led the group towards the large circular clearing. Around its edges were more of the strange rock formations that looked like cresting waves.

'Something feels strange,' said Ling-Fei as they approached. 'I can't tell if it's the power from the Ice Pearl, or something else. We should be careful.'

'And look!' said Charlotte. 'It's almost like a pattern.' It was true. The snow-packed ground spiralled inwards.

'It looks like a cinnamon bun,' said Billy. 'Man, I miss cinnamon buns.'

Ling-Fei lifted her head and focused her gaze on the centre of the clearing. 'It's there,' she said. 'The Ice Pearl. I can feel it!'

'And I think I can see it!' said Billy. 'It's glowing!' A white light rose from the middle of the clearing. Billy exhaled with relief and felt tingly with elation – they'd done it. They'd found the Ice Pearl. He'd known they could. Now all they had to do was grab the pearl and get back to the fish.

'This is weird,' said Dylan, glancing over his shoulder. 'Why would it be sitting in plain sight for anyone to take? This feels like a trap.'

'Lucky for us, I'm too fast to be caught in a trap,' said Billy. 'You guys stay here – I'll be right back.' He'd recovered now from the shock of the scorpion attack, and his levelled-up power gave him a sense of invincibility. He didn't know how or why it had strengthened, but it felt as if his whole body were thrumming with energy – as if lightning raced in his veins.

'Humble as always,' said Dylan.

Billy felt his agility and speed revving up inside him as he gauged the distance he had to run to get to the pearl.

'Be careful, Billy,' said Charlotte.

'I'll be fine,' Billy said. 'I'll grab the pearl, get back to you guys and then we'll go find the fish.'

Billy dashed as fast as he could into the centre of the clearing, his feet barely touching the ground. There, just ahead of him, was the pearl. It sat glowing in the snow, radiating pure white light from the centre of the swirls, like a jewel in a crown.

As Billy reached out to grab it, two other white pearls appeared on either side of it. Giant cloudy pearls. Weird.

Then the pearls blinked.

As Billy's hands closed round the Ice Pearl, he realized he was staring into the eyes of a huge monster.

The Wasteland Worm.

The ground beneath him began to shift as the monster uncoiled. They had been standing on it all this time.

'RUN!' Billy shouted to his friends as he leaped over the rapidly unfurling coils. 'RUN!'

The worm screeched and dived after him. He didn't look over his shoulder. He didn't need to. He could tell it was right behind him. He knew his power would allow him to outrun it, but he didn't know if the others would be able to.

'RUN!' he shouted again.

Ahead, he could see his friends stumbling, trying to get away. But they couldn't escape the clearing. The huge grey rocks had come to life all around them, and now Billy could see that they weren't rocks at all. They were giant grey worms that had been frozen in place with their mouths wide open. He had been on top of one earlier and hadn't realized. What was once white was now a sea of grey worms, slithering all around, trapping them.

'We woke them!' Ling-Fei cried. 'They were all asleep! I knew I sensed something strange.'

The Wasteland Worm was the biggest by far, but the other worms were still terrifyingly enormous and could swallow any of them whole. It was strange though – they didn't seem to be attacking, they were just circling the clearing and screeching. Only the Wasteland Worm was directly pursuing them.

Billy was almost back to his friends, which meant the Wasteland Worm would be closing in on them too.

'Just get out of here!' he yelled. 'I'll be right behind you!'

His friends were still struggling to run over the

Wasteland Worm's coiled body. They kept slipping and falling. Then, when Billy was almost with them, he saw Ling-Fei slip between two of the coils of the worm and almost disappear, only her hand still showing.

Billy lunged forward and grabbed Ling-Fei, pulling her back up.

'Billy! Look out!' he heard Charlotte scream, and he turned to see the Wasteland Worm mere centimetres away, its mouth wide open. He saw the long, sharp fangs glinting in the fading light.

He pushed Ling-Fei behind him – he knew she wouldn't be able to keep up if he started running – and he tried to think what he could do to distract the monster. Before he could make another move, the worm's giant head was yanked back.

Charlotte.

She had managed to get her arms round its thick neck, forcing it back.

'Go!' she cried. 'Get off so I can throw it!'

The Wasteland Worm thrashed in Charlotte's grip, but she held on. Billy, Dylan and Ling-Fei jumped off the last coil of the Wasteland Worm and landed in the snow. As they did, Charlotte whipped the thrashing worm in the air and slammed it on the ground. The ground shook beneath them. Still the worm thrashed and twisted its huge gaping maw, trying to get to Charlotte. She slammed it on the ground again and again, until the creature finally stopped moving and its eyes rolled back in its head. She lifted it one last time and threw it far into the distance.

The dead worm landed with a thud.

Billy had known Charlotte's power made her super-strong, but this was incredible. The other worms let out piercing screams before wriggling off into the distance, burrowing in the snow as they did.

It was strangely quiet.

'Charlotte! You did it!' Billy cried. His heart was pounding, and he was breathing hard. He couldn't believe they'd managed to escape. Charlotte had been amazing. She was still standing in the same spot, swaying a bit from side to side.

'And you frightened off the other worms too!' said Dylan. 'Well done!'

The sky began to grow dark. While they had been

running from the Wasteland Worm, the sun had started to set.

'Come on! We've got to go!' said Billy.

In the darkening sky, the strange shimmering clouds Billy had seen when they'd arrived were drawing closer. He saw now that they had long tentacles that dragged on the ground. And they were coming right towards them.

'The drifters!' he said, suddenly realizing what they were.

'Those things have an energy that is both alive and not alive,' said Ling-Fei. 'And they are hungry. We have to stay away from them!'

'Come on, Charlotte!' Dylan yelled.

But Charlotte didn't move.

'Charlotte?' Billy cried out.

She swayed again. 'I think it bit me.' She crumpled to the ground.

The Crack In The Earth

'Charlotte!' Billy ran to her. She had saved his life – he was certain of it. That worm would have swallowed him whole if she hadn't stopped it. And now she'd been bitten. She had to be okay, she just had to be. And if she wasn't . . . guilt and fear rushed through him.

'Do you still have the pearl?' Charlotte murmured, her eyes closed. 'That better not have been for nothing.'

Billy choked out a bleak laugh. 'I've got the pearl,' he said. He held it out to Dylan, who tucked it safely in his suit's secret pocket.

'Charlotte, are you okay? How do you feel?' Dylan

said, crouching next to her and Billy. Ling-Fei still stood, on alert for any other danger.

The dead worm lay still in the distance. Billy almost expected it to rear its head and charge at them again. But it stayed down. Stayed dead.

Charlotte opened one eye and stared up at the sky. 'The sun is setting,' she said. 'Y'all need to get back to that fish.'

'I think you mean "*we* all" need to get back to the fish,' said Dylan. But something in Charlotte's tone made Billy's blood run colder than the ice around them. She couldn't be saying what he thought she was.

'We're staying together,' he said firmly, taking her hand. It lay limply in his palm.

Charlotte opened her eyes and gave Billy a tight smile. 'Try to lift me,' she said. 'I can feel it already – my leg is already turning to stone. It won't be long before the rest of me turns too.'

Billy reached under Charlotte's armpits and tried to haul her up. It was no use. She was right. Her stone leg made her impossible to carry.

'I won't be able to walk on it,' she said, answering his next question. 'Even if I could, I'd turn to stone in that fish's mouth. Probably would drag it, and all of you, to the bottom of the Blood Strait.'

Ling-Fei took her gaze away from the wide-open wasteland and focused on Charlotte. She kneeled next to her friend and placed a hand on her forehead, frowning. 'It's happening fast,' she said quietly. 'If it reaches her heart, she won't make it.' Ling-Fei looked up at Billy and Dylan. 'We have to do something. Quickly.'

'Yes. Now go, before it gets dark,' said Charlotte. 'The drifters are coming. You heard what the fish said. They are more powerful at night.'

It was true. More and more of the drifters were flooding the sky, their long tentacles dragging along the ground, searching for food. Searching for them. In the evening light, they began to glow luminescent green and blue.

'I'll be all stone soon. They won't bother me.' A tear ran down Charlotte's cheek. She didn't move to wipe it away, and Billy realized she probably couldn't lift her arm.

'We're not leaving you!' he said. 'The fish said something else, remember? Something about a plant being able to save us.' He felt desperate. There had to be something they could do. They weren't going to leave Charlotte, no matter what.

'The Ember Flower,' said Dylan. 'But don't you remember what else it said? That it was far beneath the earth. Impossible for us to reach.' He glanced up. The drifters were closer now. 'Charlotte's right – we have to do something about those things soon.'

Ling-Fei stood again and put her palms together. 'Dylan, do you think your power would work on the drifters? Could you charm them?'

Dylan eyed the shifting, shimmering mass of bioluminescent blobs doubtfully. 'I don't know. I can try.'

Then Ling-Fei looked at Billy. 'Billy, you're going to have to be more agile and faster than you've been before. You won't have much time.'

'To do what?' said Billy, still holding Charlotte's hand. He squeezed it, but if she felt it she gave no sign.

'To get an Ember Flower,' Ling-Fei said. 'I think I can sense a presence beneath us. Now get ready.'

She took a step away from the group, hands still clasped, and tilted her head towards the darkening sky. The Jade Pearl started to glow beneath her protective suit, casting a green light around her.

Slowly, Ling-Fei began to pull her hands apart. She groaned, straining with the effort.

The earth beneath them groaned back.

Dylan jolted upright. 'What's happening?' he said, looking around in a panic. 'Is it an earthquake?'

Billy stared at Ling-Fei. 'I think ... Ling-Fei is opening the earth.'

And she was. With every centimetre that Ling-Fei spread her hands, the ground cracked open wider and wider. First, snow split down the middle, then the hardpacked dirt, and granite. As if in response, Dylan's Granite Pearl began to flash, joining the light of Ling-Fei's Jade Pearl. Dylan whipped his head up. 'I know what to do,' he said. 'About the drifters. I can't explain it, but my power feels stronger than ever. It's like what you said earlier, Billy, about your power levelling up. It's happening to me too. I think you are right – it has to do with how long we've had the pearls, but it is more than that. I think, when we feel the need to protect one another, our power gets some sort of boost.' He turned his attention to the drifters creeping ever closer in the sky above them.

Suddenly, a mirror image of the four friends appeared directly beneath the drifters. A large drifter halted, its tentacles clawing at the ground below it, through the mirage, at the stones beneath. It was enough to keep the creature occupied. Other drifters were drawn to the commotion and some turned back – away from where the real children were, floating to the conjured image.

'Whoa,' breathed Billy.

'My brain feels as if it is about to spill out of my nose, to be honest,' said Dylan through gritted teeth. 'I don't know how long I can keep this up.'

'Keep what up?' said Charlotte.

'Dylan is distracting the drifters,' said Billy. 'And Ling-Fei has opened the earth. We are going to save you. I promise.' He looked over at the widening crack in the ground. It was steaming now, and Billy glimpsed an orange glow emanating from deep within. Ling-Fei had opened the earth deep enough to where the Ember Flower grew. And still she pulled her hands wider apart.

'Now, Billy!' she yelled. 'I can't hold it open much longer.'

Billy squeezed Charlotte's hand again. 'All you need to do is stay awake, okay? Can you do that?'

'I'll try,' said Charlotte. 'Be careful.'

As Billy stared into the belly of the earth, his Lightning Pearl began to flicker and spark. A sense of calm descended on him, and a sureness spread through his limbs. He could do this.

'I'm going in!' he shouted. 'Stay together!' Before he could think too much about it, he leaped into the crack in the earth and disappeared.

The Ember Flower

Billy let himself fall deeper and deeper inside the earth. He was going incredibly fast, but he felt in total control.

It was hot, almost unbearably so. The crack was narrow, only as wide as Ling-Fei could hold it apart, and sharp rocks on the sides would have ripped him open if he hadn't been wearing his suit. He fell down, down, down and then his vision zoned in on something.

A faint red glow flickering far beneath him. That had to be it.

The Ember Flower.

Billy flung his arms out, his hands dragging along the sides of the crack in the earth, the friction slowing him to a stop. He clung to the wall and looked at his hands. They should have had the skin scraped off. They should be burning from the heat. But he didn't feel any pain. Instead, they were fizzing all over with electricity from the Lightning Pearl, almost like a pair of protective electric gloves. He guessed that his face was covered in the same kind of electric mask.

But, even with the Lightning Pearl's protection, he didn't have much time. The walls around him shuddered. Ling-Fei was struggling to keep the crack open.

Very carefully, he climbed lower, his feet somehow knowing exactly where to go, until he reached where the Ember Flower grew out of the rock.

It had red and gold petals that glowed like molten coals and inside a fire flickered. When he looked around, he could see there were more of them, sprouting deep within the earth, like a field of Ember Flowers. With trembling hands, he gently plucked one, grateful for his protected hands.

He heard a distant cry from far above.

'Hurry, Billy!'

His mind whizzed through the possibilities of

what could be happening up there. Maybe Charlotte had turned completely to stone. Or the drifters were about to eat them. Or Ling-Fei couldn't hold the crack open any longer.

He had to get back to his friends. They were all depending on him.

But then Billy realized that, even with his pearl powers of agility and speed, he needed both hands to scramble back up the tunnel to above ground. He blew tentatively on the Ember Flower, desperately hoping the fire inside wouldn't go out. It didn't.

'This had better work,' he said out loud, before placing the stem carefully between his teeth.

The walls around him juddered violently. It was time to move.

He shot up the crevice, using the walls like a ladder, leaping from one rock crack to the other as fast as he could. When it was too far for him to leap, even with his power, he climbed the rock face like a spider until he could jump again. And still the Ember Flower glowed. He tried not to notice how small a space he was in, how the walls seemed to be closing in with each passing second. How they probably *were* closing in because Ling-Fei could only hold the earth open for so long.

The sky far above was growing darker. He heard Dylan shout, so he pushed himself to go faster, kicking off the ledges as hard as he could until he was almost at the top.

The walls were closing rapidly round him now, pressing against his shoulders.

With a last burst of energy, he kicked off a ledge one last time, and his hands clawed at solid ground.

Dylan was there in an instant, grabbing Billy's arms and pulling him out. 'Took you long enough, didn't it?' he said. 'Those things have figured out my trick, and they're faster than they look.' Behind him the drifters were edging ever closer, their tentacles sweeping the ground hungrily.

As soon as Billy was out of the crevice, Ling-Fei's hands slammed shut, and the earth closed with a thundering crash. The ground rocked for a moment, then stilled.

Ling-Fei collapsed next to Charlotte. 'Is that it?' she panted. Billy reached up and took the Ember Flower from between his teeth. It still glowed.

Charlotte's eyes were closed, and he could see now that her hands had turned to stone too. He desperately hoped it hadn't reached her heart yet – that he'd found the Ember Flower in time. He couldn't imagine their group without Charlotte. They needed her, and not just for her dragon bond and pearl. She was their friend too.

Ling-Fei and Dylan gently propped up Charlotte's head. Her eyes fluttered open.

'You made it,' she rasped.

'I did,' said Billy. He held the Ember Flower out. Now that he had it here, he wasn't quite sure what to do.

'The fish said something about the breath,' said Dylan. 'Maybe she . . . smells it?'

'That's it,' said Billy, the realization clicking. 'Here, Charlotte, breathe in through your nose – there you go, like that.'

Charlotte inhaled deeply, once, twice, and on the third time she began to cough. 'It's so hot,' she said, her voice hoarse. 'It's burning me!'

'That's good,' said Billy soothingly, even though he had no idea whether it was supposed to do that.

'Billy's right,' said Ling-Fei, watching Charlotte closely. 'The stone, it's disappearing. You are more you already!'

She was right. Billy gazed in amazement as Charlotte's stone hands slowly turned to skin. It looked as if the grey stone were being erased from her body one smudge at a time, until only her skin remained. What was moments earlier frozen in place was now limber with life once more.

Charlotte clenched and unclenched her fist and began to grin. 'I can feel my fingers again!'

'Keep smelling the Ember Flower,' said Billy.

'And, as soon as you think you can get up and move, let us know,' said Dylan. Then he muttered quietly to Billy, 'We're running out of time.'

Billy glanced up at the sky. He'd been so focused on finding the Ember Flower he hadn't noticed the sun had disappeared.

'The fish will be gone,' he murmured to Dylan.

'I'm not worried about the fish right now, I'm worried about those things,' said Dylan, pointing at the horde of drifters almost on top of them.

To Billy's horror, he saw one tentacle scuttle across

to a small rodent-type creature on the ice. The drifter paused and the tentacle went taut. Then, like a giant straw, it slurped up the blood, intestines and finally the skin of the rodent, leaving only the bones on the ice.

Dylan gulped audibly. 'That answers the question about where all those bones came from. I don't think I have the strength to trick them again. Of all the ways to die, I did not think having my insides sucked up by huge floating jellyfish monsters was how I was going to go, but here we are.'

'We are not going to die!' Billy said emphatically. 'We've come too far!'

'Billy's right,' said Charlotte. 'You didn't save me for nothing. I didn't almost turn to stone to die by tentacle right after.' With Ling-Fei's help, she stood up. 'And there is no way I'm letting these floating, brainless blobs be the end of me.'

'As always, I love your optimism, but in case you haven't noticed we're surrounded,' said Dylan.

The drifters were floating towards them from every direction now.

'Even if the fish had, by some miracle, decided to wait for us, we couldn't get to it,' Dylan went on.

'Maybe we can burrow beneath the snow?' said Ling-Fei. 'Like the worms?'

'We can try,' said Dylan, his voice cracking.

'The worms would get us underneath the snow,' said Charlotte. 'And I'm too weak to fight them off now.'

The group huddled together as the drifters came closer, closer, closer. They were trapped. There was no escape.

The Power Of A Pearl

The drifters were almost upon them. Billy tensed, waiting to be struck by one of their tentacles.

Please, Spark – help us, he thought desperately.

Nothing.

He remembered what the dragons had said: they couldn't help them while they were in the Frozen Wasteland.

Billy and his friends were on their own.

Billy, Charlotte, Ling-Fei and Dylan huddled in a tight circle, their shoulders all touching as they looked at each other's faces for what was probably the last time. At least they were together.

'Wait,' Billy said. 'I've got an idea.'

'It'd better be a good one,' said Dylan.

'And it'd better be fast,' added Charlotte. 'Those things are moving in.'

'Well?' added Ling-Fei, nudging Billy. 'What is the idea?'

Billy's thoughts were all in a jumble, but he tried to focus. 'Do you remember when Spark made the portal out of her hoard?'

'I don't remember as I wasn't there, if you recall?' said Dylan.

'Not the point, Dylan,' said Charlotte. 'And, Billy, we don't have a handy dragon hoard or a dragon nearby to make a portal!'

'I think Billy is onto something,' said Ling-Fei, eyes bright.

'Spark said that to power the portal it needed energy, magic and sacrifice. We've got magic, with our pearls. And I think we can transfer some of our energy, this fear and adrenaline we're feeling, into it, so all we need is a sacrifice.'

'Volunteering yourself, are you?' said Dylan. 'Also, if we are going to do something, we seriously need to do it fast.'

'We can't sacrifice the pearls, we need them, but we've got to have something worth sacrificing. Something that would belong in a dragon hoard – special enough to generate that kind of power.'

'My ring!' said Dylan, tugging it off. 'It would definitely belong in my hoard if I had one. It is the most precious thing to me.' He looked at it in his palm. 'It saved me once before – I bet it can save us now.' Then he swallowed. 'I hope, if we ever get home, my granddad won't be too mad that I lost it.'

Charlotte reached out and squeezed his hand. 'I'm sure he will understand. Saving the world and all that takes sacrifice sometimes.' Then she frowned. 'But where do we put the ring?'

'I've got that,' said Ling-Fei. 'Back up.' She stared hard at the ice in front of them and, moments later, a small pool of water appeared, large enough for them all to step into.

Suddenly, the Lightning Pearl grew hot beneath the collar of Billy's protective suit. It was so hot against his skin, he couldn't stand it. He yanked it out, and saw his friends doing the same. The pearls flashed, and a burst of energy shot out from each of them, shining onto the pool Ling-Fei had created. It began to glow. 'Whoa,' said Dylan. 'Do we really think this is going to work?'

'I think it's our best shot,' said Billy. 'Spark's portal pulled us to this time because we all had a connection to you. And we've all got a connection to our dragons, so hopefully this portal will take us to them. We have to try.'

Dylan dropped his ring in the pool. It began to whirl faster and faster. Billy felt a slippery tentacle on his shoulder and a sharp shot of pain went through him. 'Now!' he yelled. 'Use the bond!'

Holding hands, the four friends jumped in feet first with no idea where they would end up. As the portal pulled them in, Billy glanced back and saw the end of a tentacle probe where he had just been standing. Then everything went bright white, and he felt as if he were being squeezed through a tube of toothpaste. All he could focus on was holding onto Charlotte's and Ling-Fei's hands. He couldn't let go of them, he had to hold on . . .

*

Suddenly, they were out of the portal and falling through the air, still clutching hands. They'd done it. They'd made a portal and jumped through it. Billy just hoped they had jumped to safety and not somewhere worse than where they'd been. His head pounded and he tried to stand, but couldn't. And then their dragons were there, catching them and carrying them to the edge of a lake. Billy lay in Spark's arms, still feeling dizzy from the portal jump. The experience was even worse than the first time.

'How did they get here?' he heard Tank say.

'They must have used the pearls somehow,' said Spark. Spark! Billy was glad to hear her voice. 'There is still so much we don't know about the power of the pearls.'

'The children are unwell. Whatever they did took a toll on them,' said Buttons, sounding concerned.

'We do not have time for them to be sick,' said Xing. 'The Diamond Pearl is close.'

'I will heal them,' said Buttons. 'Bring them here.'

Billy was vaguely aware of curling up in front of Buttons, and then the familiar lull of the dragon's singing washed over him.

Billy wasn't sure if minutes or hours had passed, but his head cleared and his body felt strong again. He felt as if he'd had a full night's sleep, although the sky was still dark and the moons were high.

He blinked and looked for Spark. She was staring down at him. Her eyes were gold and clear, as they should be. He breathed a sigh of relief.

'I never want to be separated from Tank ever again,' said Charlotte, hugging her dragon's front claw.

'I'm glad you are back with us too,' said Tank. Billy wasn't completely sure, but he thought Tank looked . . . emotional. Or at least as emotional as a gigantic red warrior dragon could.

'How long were we asleep?' said Dylan, yawning and stretching his arms over his head.

'Mere moments,' said Xing. 'Buttons used his healing power, and it worked wonders. You could barely stand when you came barrelling out of that portal.'

'It was very unpleasant,' said Ling-Fei. 'As was the Frozen Wasteland.'

'Ling-Fei opened the earth with her hands,' Billy blurted out. 'And Charlotte threw the Wasteland

Worm into the ground so hard it died, but not before it bit her. She almost turned to stone. And Dylan conjured images of us so the drifters wouldn't suck our insides out.'

'And Billy went inside the earth to find the Ember Flower to save my life,' said Charlotte.

'We saved each other,' said Billy.

The dragons stilled. 'We did not realize how much danger we would be putting you in,' said Spark. 'I am sorry. But I am also not surprised that you survived by working together. That must have been how you created a portal to bring you to safety. It is the four of you – you have bonds with us, but also with one another. There is magic working together. After all, that is how you opened the mountain and saved us.'

Billy looked at his friends and was filled with so much pride he thought he might burst.

'There's something else too,' said Ling-Fei. 'Our powers seem to be growing stronger.'

'Interesting,' said Xing. 'I suspect it has something to do with the length of time you've been wearing the pearls. But, as Spark said earlier, there is much we don't know about the power of the pearl.'

'Adding to our rapidly expanding list of near-death experiences – that fish almost ate us,' said Dylan. 'Thank goodness Billy had that soul coin.'

'A shame you no longer have it,' said Xing.

'It was the soul coin or one of us,' said Billy. 'It seemed like the right decision.'

'I wish we didn't have to go so quickly, but we can't let all your hard work be for nothing,' said Buttons. 'Xing has sensed the Diamond Pearl. We must get it.'

Everyone turned their gaze on Xing.

'It is in the Human Realm,' said Xing. 'And there is a door between the realms in this lake.'

The Lake Between Realms

'There are other humans in this time?' said Billy, eyeing the lake. He realized he actually had no idea what time they were in. It hadn't seemed to matter in the Dragon Realm, since it was all so strange and alien to them already.

'Apparently so,' said Xing.

'I guess we shouldn't be so surprised. The dragons who gave us the soul coin had clearly seen humans before. And so had the giant fish,' said Ling-Fei.

'Hold on,' said Dylan. 'What if we accidentally change the course of human history? What if I see my great-great-great-great-granddad or something and say or do something that means he doesn't meet my great-great-great-great-grandma and then I disappear? I've seen that movie! I don't want to star in it!'

'This entrance is leading us into what you know as China. I sincerely doubt you'll stumble upon *your* ancestors there,' said Xing.

'There are realm entrances into where you come from too though,' said Buttons quietly. 'I've seen your country. It is very green. Which is, as you might not be surprised to know, my favourite colour.'

'Dragons in Ireland,' said Dylan, shaking his head. 'Just when I think I've got a handle on all this.'

'What about me and Ling-Fei?' said Billy. 'We might see *our* ancestors in China, right?'

'If we do this correctly, you won't interact with anyone,' said Xing. 'You found the Lightning Pearl without detection, so surely this won't be much more difficult.'

Another thought occurred to Billy. 'But have we messed up your timeline? Here in the Dragon Realm?'

'Dragons travel through time more often than humans; our timelines are always shifting. Do not worry,' said Tank.

'And after we find this pearl . . . we face the Dragon of Death?' said Billy. He swallowed nervously. The Wasteland Worm had nearly finished them – how could they take on the Dragon of Death herself?

'Yes,' said Tank. 'And we make sure she can never return to our time or any other. Now we will be able to defeat her.' He paused. 'Although we should probably tell you that she cannot be killed. She is immortal.'

'What?' said Dylan. 'That would have been good to know before we decided we would take her on!'

'There are ways of defeating her other than death,' said Xing.

'How is it even possible for her to be immortal?' said Ling-Fei.

'Legend has it that she ate one of the peaches of immortality. But nobody knows for certain. All we know now is she cannot die, and death is part of who she is,' said Buttons.

'But do not be discouraged by this,' said Tank. 'We are so much stronger now with the four of you, and you four are growing increasingly powerful the more you work together and the longer the pearls are in your possession. She will be no match for us.'

'She's probably bonded with Old Gold though,' said Ling-Fei. 'Won't that mean she's much stronger too?'

'And the fact that she is *immortal*,' muttered Dylan.

'Immortal does not mean invincible,' said Xing.

Billy hoped Xing was right. Then he noticed how quiet Spark was being. And he sensed a strange anxiety emanating from her.

Are you okay? he thought down their bond. She didn't reply, and he pushed again. *Spark?*

I'm fine, she replied finally. And then her thoughts flowed fast and strong, almost overwhelming Billy. *I worry we may be underestimating the Dragon of Death. She is very powerful. The dark magic in this land is growing stronger by the day. We will have to be very strong to defeat her.* Spark went quiet again.

Billy didn't feel reassured by this. It was a new sensation, having to be strong for his dragon. *We are strong*, he thought back with as much optimism as he could muster.

And then, to make it clear how much he believed in Spark and their dragons, how much he believed in all of them, he spoke out loud too. 'Tank is right. We've got this.'

'And then we can go home,' sighed Dylan wistfully. 'Sleep in a real bed! Eat something other than fish or peaches!' He looked around at the dragons. 'I'm very grateful for the fish and peaches, of course.'

'I hope everyone is okay back at camp. I bet they're worried about us. And about Old Gold,' said Ling-Fei thoughtfully.

'How . . . how long have we been gone?' asked Billy. 'I've lost track.' Remembering home hit him like a punch in the gut. He hoped his parents had at least received his note.

'Time works differently here,' Spark said gently. 'It isn't easy to know how much time has passed in your realm.'

'And you'll be back soon,' added Buttons.

'All the more reason to move quickly,' said Xing. 'The sooner we find this pearl and defeat the Dragon of Death, the sooner we can go back to our own time.'

'Xing is right,' said Tank. 'Now, we don't know how deep the lake goes. You may not be able to hold your breath as long as you need to . . .'

'That is in no way comforting,' said Dylan.

'I can hold my breath for a very long time,' said Charlotte. 'I'll be fine.'

'Oh, grand,' said Dylan. 'Never mind the rest of us.'

'As I was saying,' said Tank, 'you may not be able to hold your breath, so we will take precautions. As soon as we are underwater, Xing will blow air bubbles round your heads. They will not last for ever, so take as few breaths as you can.'

Billy was a good swimmer – at home he spent most of his free time surfing after all – but the idea of deliberately diving to the bottom of a deep lake made his chest hurt. He reminded himself he knew how to hold his breath, and he knew how to stay calm. This was about saving the world. It mattered more than anything.

'And be sure to hold on tight,' added Buttons.

'Good thing I'm not stone any more,' Charlotte said with a wry grin.

'When we emerge, we will be in the Human Realm. Are you ready?' said Tank.

Don't worry, Spark thought to Billy. *I won't let anything happen to you.*

*

The lake reflected the purple sky, stars winking above and around them as the dragons lowered themselves into the water.

When they were fully submerged, Xing blew a stream of air at each of them, and an air bubble secured over their heads. Billy felt a bit like an astronaut. An astronaut riding a dragon underwater.

He allowed himself a small breath. And then another. He really could breathe in the bubble. And he could see out of it as well. Strange plant life waved beneath them, flickering in the dark.

The dragons did not seem to need air bubbles. Billy wasn't sure if they were holding their breath or if they could breathe underwater too.

They dived deeper and deeper into the lake until something like a shimmering curtain appeared in front of them. They swam through it, and as they did Billy felt a tingle run over his whole body. He knew that they had passed back into the Human Realm. What he didn't know was what they would find there.

Legend Of The Four Dragons

They swam up, up and up and then the dragons and their riders burst out of the lake and into the Human Realm.

As soon as they were out of the water, the air bubble around Billy's head popped, and he gulped in fresh air.

Are you all right? Spark asked. *Crossing realms is not always pleasant.*

That was a piece of cake compared to going through a portal, Billy thought back.

I have never had cake. Perhaps after this is all over you can arrange for me to try some.

Billy grinned. *Definitely. Vanilla cake with*

chocolate frosting. He paused, thinking. Might there really be a time he could share cake with Spark? He hoped so. They were so close now. They just needed that last pearl.

He looked down at the lake they had emerged from. It appeared perfectly normal – no sign that it was really a secret entrance to another realm. 'I feel like we might have just solved the mystery of the Loch Ness monster,' he said.

'Oh, yeah. Definitely a dragon,' said Dylan. 'Loch Ness must be an entrance between realms too. I wonder how many there are in the world.'

'Fewer than there used to be,' said Buttons.

'It's beautiful here,' said Ling-Fei, gazing around in wonder.

The lake sat amid lush green hills, like soup in a bowl. In the golden light of the rising sun, Billy noticed something cutting across the top of the hills above them.

He rubbed his eyes. 'Is that ... the Great Wall of China?'

'Holy pecan pie, I think you're right!' said Charlotte. 'That kind of helps us narrow down when we are, but not much. The wall was built so long ago!'

'We'll know more soon,' said Xing. 'I suspect the Diamond Pearl is in human hands. Come, let's fly closer.'

'What if someone looks up?' said Dylan. 'We aren't exactly . . . subtle.'

'It is early. If anything, we may only frighten some farmers. It has happened before,' said Tank.

'And I guess in this time we don't need to worry about being knocked out of the sky by a missile or anything,' said Billy.

'Precisely. But we must still go carefully – humans have a surprising skill for violence. Especially when they feel threatened,' said Buttons.

'Well, I still think we'd win,' said Charlotte, patting Tank. 'Tank could take on anyone or anything.'

'I appreciate your confidence,' said Tank. 'But let us not dwell on the idea of being discovered and instead hope for the best.'

'That is surprisingly optimistic of you,' said Dylan.

'You humans seem to make me more hopeful,' Tank grumbled.

*

The sun was now high in a bright blue sky. Billy felt as if the familiar round sun were an old friend. They weren't back in their own time, but they were in their own world, and it felt nice. It gave him hope that they really would be able to return home after all this.

Xing and Ling-Fei led the way, following her sense of the Diamond Pearl. As they flew, they stayed near the Great Wall, sometimes flying directly over it. Billy stared in amazement as it went on and on, undulating over the hills. Even after all the wonders he had seen in the Dragon Realm, he was awed by the sheer scale of the Great Wall. He realized that nobody except the three other people he was with would ever be able to see it the way he was, soaring over on the back of a dragon. In that moment, all his fear and anxiety about what lay ahead vanished, and only his amazement remained. He felt indescribably lucky. He wished he could share it with his parents and his brother. The idea of his parents riding a dragon almost made him laugh out loud.

'What are you smiling about?' asked Charlotte, who was flying next to him.

'This view,' said Billy.

'Humans are capable of amazing things,' Spark said.

They flew on until a huge fortress rose up in the distance.

'There,' said Xing. 'The Diamond Pearl is in there.'

'That must be the Imperial Palace,' said Ling-Fei. 'I bet the emperor has the Diamond Pearl.'

'And *I* bet he will be heavily guarded. Do you see the walls on that place?' said Dylan. 'How are we even going to get in?'

'Come on, Dylan,' said Billy. 'You conjured an illusion of the four of us in the Frozen Wasteland. We defeated a giant worm. We can handle a few guards.' This was going to be the easy part. No terrifying Dragon Realm creatures to worry about. Just humans. They could handle humans.

'I have a feeling it is going to be more than a few guards,' said Dylan.

'Good thing we've got dragons on our side,' said Charlotte.

'I don't want them to get hurt,' said Ling-Fei.

'We'll be fine,' said Spark. 'Charlotte is right. We

are the perfect distraction. Let us give them a show they will be talking about for centuries.'

'An excellent plan. How else will they know how magnificent we are? Let us start the Legend of the Four Dragons today,' said Xing.

Tank roared his approval.

'So we're not taking the whole "don't be seen" approach,' said Dylan.

'*We* will be seen. You four will sneak into the palace and find the Diamond Pearl. It is a simple plan. Even you should be able to comprehend it,' said Xing.

'Our simple plans never seem to stay simple,' said Dylan. 'But who am I to stop the Legend of the Four Dragons?'

'That's the spirit,' said Billy. 'To the palace!'

The Imperial Palace

The Imperial Palace was bigger than any building Billy had ever seen. It wasn't even one building. As they flew closer, Billy saw that the outer perimeter contained at least a dozen buildings, all connected by courtyards and walkways. The centre of the palace rose up like a layer cake, with stairs connecting the different levels.

The palace sat within sight of the Great Wall, but not too close. There was a tall watchtower in each of the four corners of the complex. Billy felt certain that the guards in those towers had never seen what was approaching the palace now.

'Shall we say hello?' said Tank, and he shot a massive plume of fire into the air.

Spark's wings crackled with electricity, and Xing flew in figures of eight in the sky. Buttons roared.

It had an immediate effect. Guards began shouting and running around. One fired a crossbow in the direction of the dragons before the others stopped him, knocking him to the ground.

'This emperor will be seen as blessed because we have deigned to visit him,' said Xing. 'We bring good fortune, you know.'

'Look!' said Ling-Fei, pointing. 'I think that's the emperor, right there!'

The figure walking down one of the central sets of stairs wore flowing robes of blue and gold. He had a long, pointed black beard, visible even from the sky. On his head was a tall and elaborate headdress. As he paused to look up, Billy noticed something sparkling in the centre of the headdress.

The Diamond Pearl.

'It's in his hat!' Billy said. 'I can see it!'

'How are we going to get to him?' said Dylan. 'He's surrounded by courtiers and guards!'

It was true. The emperor was closely followed by

courtiers wearing smaller blue hats. Behind them were guards carrying crossbows.

'The dragons are doing a great job of distracting everyone, but we would need to be invisible to get to that darn pearl,' said Charlotte.

Invisible. 'I've got an idea!' Billy shouted. 'Dylan, you know how you conjured the image of us to the drifters, using your charm?'

Dylan nodded.

'What if you conjure air where we are?'

'You want me to make us *invisible*?' said Dylan, looking pale.

'You need to make your plan soon,' said Tank. 'We're almost at the palace.'

'You can do it,' said Billy. 'I believe in you, Dylan.'

'Okay,' said Dylan, although he didn't sound confident.

'Come on, Dylan!' said Charlotte. 'You've got this!'

Dylan closed his eyes tightly for a moment. When he opened them, Billy looked down at his own hand.

He couldn't see it.

'It worked!' cried Dylan. 'At least, I think it worked! Unless you three fell off your dragons?'

'It worked,' came Ling-Fei's disembodied voice from Xing's back.

'I can't get it to work on myself though,' said Dylan. 'And I don't know how long I can keep it up.' A bead of sweat dripped down his brow. 'It's really hard.'

'Dylan and I will stay up high so he isn't seen by any of the humans. You three, go quickly,' said Buttons.

'Billy, Charlotte, jump on my back,' said Xing. 'I'll take you two and Ling-Fei to the emperor and then fly back up here. He'll be so stunned by my appearance it will be the perfect time to take the pearl.'

'And, Billy, your agility skill makes you the perfect person to take it,' added Spark as Billy hopped off her back and onto Xing's easily. Billy nodded, and pride bloomed in his chest. He felt ready for anything. He could do this.

'And, if anything goes wrong or anyone gets too close, I'll punch our way out,' said Charlotte.

'Your go-to response,' said Billy.

'Hey, it's worked so far, hasn't it?' said Charlotte, and, even though Billy couldn't see her, he could have sworn she was smiling.

'You may need more than brute strength,' said Xing as they flew down into the palace. 'Which is where Ling-Fei will be helpful.'

As Xing landed gracefully in the courtyard, all the humans around her dropped to their knees and a hush fell over them.

Only the emperor remained standing.

'Go quickly,' hissed Xing.

Moving as fast as he could, Billy hopped over two kneeling guards and landed deftly in front of the emperor. The emperor stared straight through him, captivated by Xing.

With trembling fingers, Billy reached out and tugged on the Diamond Pearl. It emitted a shining glow, so bright he couldn't look directly at it. The pearl stayed stuck on the emperor's hat.

'Hurry.' Charlotte's voice was suddenly in his ear.

With another sharp pull, the Diamond Pearl fell loose from the headdress and landed in Billy's invisible hand.

Before anyone could spot the pearl floating in mid-air, he tucked it into his suit.

He moved closer to Xing, edging between two

guards to reach her. 'Let's get out of here,' he said quietly, hoping Ling-Fei and Charlotte were close enough to hear him. They'd done it. They had the Diamond Pearl.

And then the guard behind him burst into flames.

A Noxious Arrival

Billy had never seen anyone die before. It was awful. The man was screaming and Billy could smell his charred skin. Something had gone terribly wrong. Their dragons wouldn't attack a human like that for no reason.

'Billy! I can see you!' shouted Charlotte. 'Dylan's power isn't working! And that guy is on fire! What is happening?'

'I can see you too!' said Billy, as Charlotte and Ling-Fei shimmered back into existence. 'This is bad – really bad!'

The guards started shouting and raising their crossbows.

'Don't hurt us,' Ling-Fei said quickly in Chinese. 'We're—'

Before she could finish her sentence, Xing interrupted, 'Quick! Get on my back! We need to get out of here!'

Billy, Charlotte and Ling-Fei scrambled onto Xing's back as arrows began flying through the air around them. Billy stared up at the sky in horror.

The Dragon of Death.

Billy knew it was the Dragon of Death before he saw her. He could feel her presence in the air around him, and a chill crept through his bones and gripped his heart. He could feel her power, and he could tell that Spark felt it too. Looking up, Billy saw the most beautiful and fearsome creature he'd ever seen. The dragon's scales were shimmering black and deep purple. Long, slender spikes went all the way down her spine, and two black curved horns sat atop her head like a crown. Her eyes glowed blood-red, and she was enveloped in an aurora of purple light that seeped out from beneath her scales.

The dragon threw her head back and roared, revealing rows and rows of jagged black teeth.

'Humans! Bow before me!' Her voice was icy and penetrating. It was the voice of someone who was always obeyed. She turned her gaze on Tank, Spark, Xing and Buttons. 'We meet again, I see. Now it is time for you to accept me as your true ruler.'

'We will never join you!' Tank roared back. 'I would die before I would let you come to power. We banished you once, and we will do so again. You should have stayed where we sent you.'

'My greatness cannot be contained!' The Dragon of Death's voice echoed all around them.

Billy noticed that Old Gold wasn't on her back. He wondered briefly if something had happened to him, and then, with a gust of wind, there he was, flying on a cloud and carrying a staff. His white beard was longer, and his eyes shone with malice and power.

'You foolish children!' he yelled. 'Stop getting in our way!'

He waved his staff and the wind began to rush at them.

'The Flaming Pearl and his bond with the Dragon of Death have turned him into a sorcerer!' cried Ling-Fei.

Three nox-wing dragons appeared in the air and flew round the Dragon of Death. They were smaller than her, but looked almost as formidable. One was striped in shades of midnight blue with huge wings and a long spike at the end of its tail. The other two dragons were a steel grey and had long, slender bodies like Xing.

The humans below them scattered and screamed at the sight of the Dragon of Death and the nox-wings. The emperor stared up at them, seemingly frozen in awe and terror, and his guards closed in around him, shooting arrows at both the nox-wing dragons and Spark and the others. The dragons barely noticed the arrows, only swatting them away when they came close to their human riders.

Then another, more familiar, dragon emerged from the clouds.

It was Dimitrius. And he had a human on his back. Billy squinted as the figure came into sight. Was that . . . JJ? It couldn't be. But it was.

JJ was flying on Dimitrius's back.

Billy gasped. Dimitrius had led the nox-wings' mission to bring back the Dragon of Death, and he had devastated the Dragon Realm in order to do so, taking life force from good dragons and killing those that got in their way. They'd defeated him once before and had not expected to see him in this time. Especially not with JJ. Billy felt the sharp prick of betrayal. He should have known JJ would have sided with his grandfather. Even so, it hurt. Dimitrius swooped next to the Dragon of Death and laughed in the direction of Billy and the others. 'Well, well, well. We meet again.'

'Am I seeing things?' said Charlotte. 'How the heck did Dimitrius get here?'

'You fools left that portal into the past wide open! Did you not think I would come looking for you? Looking for the Great One? That I was just going to crawl off and disappear for ever? No, I went right to your precious mountain. And imagine my delight when I saw a portal, waiting for me to jump into it. Your enchantments may have been strong enough to keep most dragons from finding it, but for me they were nothing.' Dimitrius blew flames towards Spark. 'It was quite impressive, I will concede. I am surprised you were able to create such a thing. I'll admit that is beyond even my capability.'

Billy knew that Dimitrius was referring to the fact that Spark would have had to use dark magic to open the portal. And it made his skin prickle, thinking about his dragon having anything in common with Dimitrius and the nox-wings.

'But it wasn't strong enough. It broke when I travelled through it – or else I could have brought the Great One back to our time to begin her glorious rule. No matter, we will win here and now, and wipe you from existence. And what difference does it make if we conquer humans now or in the future? Our lives are long.' Dimitrius flashed an evil grin, his eyes glinting. 'And I've found a human with a heart to match my own. A human with a pearl.'

Billy could see now that Dimitrius looked even bigger and stronger than when they'd last seen him. His claws were longer, sharper. The massive horns on his head had grown and looked as if they'd been forged in fire, still glowing bright and molten from the heat. His bond with JJ must have boosted his strength, as it had their dragons when they had bonded with them.

Billy bit back the fear rising in his stomach. 'JJ,

what are you doing? You belong with us! Not with Dimitrius.' He had wanted to believe the best of JJ. But how could JJ have bonded with someone as evil as Dimitrius if he didn't have a heart that matched?

'I told you, Billy Chan, we were never meant to be friends,' said JJ. 'And this isn't Dimitrius. His name is Da Huo, and he is my dragon.' Billy recognized that the name meant 'big fire' in Mandarin. 'Now I've got a dragon and the Coral Pearl too,' JJ went on. 'You aren't so special any more.'

'It doesn't need to be like this!' pleaded Billy, trying to convince himself as much as JJ. If there was still a chance that JJ would join them, would fight alongside them against the Dragon of Death, he would try. Maybe it wasn't too late.

'Oh, but it does!' said Old Gold. 'My grandson is right where he should be. On the side of victory and greatness.'

'You are a rotten soul!' shouted Ling-Fei. 'And you will never win!' Her voice was trembling, but her chin was high.

'I grow weary of this reunion,' said the Dragon of Death, her icy voice cutting through the air, silencing them all. 'I'll ask one last time because I am in a generous mood. Join me.'

'Never!' Billy cried. He was trembling from the nearness of the Dragon of Death.

Charlotte, Dylan and Ling-Fei all shouted in agreement, and their dragons bared their teeth and growled. It was always going to come to this. A battle for the ages.

'Very well,' said the Dragon of Death. 'I will enjoy taking your lives, along with your pearls. Nox-wings! Take no prisoners!'

The dragon they had known as Dimitrius roared and charged. Tank leaped towards him, Charlotte on his back, their bond keeping them together while they flew through the air at an impossible speed.

They crashed into each other with a thunderous *boom*. Da Huo swung his molten horns at Tank, who dodged backwards a moment too late. Billy watched in horror as the points of Da Huo's horns slashed across Tank's chest and cut right through his thick, armoured scales. Tank let out a cry of pain.

Da Huo took the chance to lunge at Tank's throat. Tank must have been expecting this as he spun out of the way, swinging his massive tail and whipping it across Da Huo's face with a heavy crack. Da Huo's body went limp and he fell, head first, out of the sky. Tank swooped down and clamped his teeth on the falling dragon's tail and spun him round in circles, gathering more and more speed before launching Da Huo, with JJ still on his back, towards the Great Wall. The huge dragon crashed through it, sending debris everywhere, but not before JJ leaped off with incredible speed.

With a jolt, Billy realized that JJ's pearl powers must be similar to his own. The pearl had unlocked some kind of super-speed within JJ, and Billy wondered what other new abilities he had.

The three other nox-wings turned their attention to the palace and shot enormous jets of fire at Billy and the others, but, before the flames reached them, Xing blocked their efforts with a tidal wave of frost and ice. The fire and ice collided in mid-air, setting off an explosion that shook the earth.

Old Gold raised his staff and pointed it at the palace, his eyes flashing purple.

The guards' crossbows pulled away from

their owners. Arrows slotted themselves in the bows' chambers.

'Watch out!' Billy cried.

Ling-Fei flung her arms out, throwing a vicious jet of wind at Old Gold. The cloud beneath his feet swayed violently, sending the old man off balance. The crossbows fell to the ground.

The Dragon of Death laughed again. 'That is a nifty trick, little girl.' A nasty smirk touched her lips. 'Enjoy these next breaths. They will be your last.'

Battle In The Sky

The Dragon of Death straightened her long body and flapped her wings furiously. The purple gas seeping beneath her scales began to billow out in huge clouds, and soon she was almost enveloped in a toxic purple fog. She took a huge breath, sucking in all the fog. Then her eyes turned from red to black as she unhinged her jaw and let out a sea of purple noxious gas that rushed at Billy and the others like an avalanche.

'Buttons, protect us!' yelled Tank, who had rejoined the group.

Buttons threw up his arms as the mass of purple was about to hit them, forming a protective shield.

The gas parted round the shield, keeping Billy and his friends safe inside. But not before Billy saw that the emperor and his guards didn't have anything to protect them.

He watched in horror as the palace residents were shrouded in a cloud of purple that seemed to have a mind of its own. Tendrils forced their way into eyes and mouths and also into the palace behind them. Billy watched as the emperor was afflicted, hundreds of raised bumps forming under the skin of his face and hands, crawling around like beetles under a rug. The emperor scratched at his eyes, yelling in agony, before falling to his knees. His body writhed in pain. It looked as if he were being eaten alive from the inside. Billy's stomach clenched with terror and he thought he might be sick.

Ling-Fei gasped, panic in her eyes. 'We have to save them!'

'She is sucking out their life force,' said Xing. 'She will be even more powerful than she is now – human life force is especially strong.'

Billy was scared. This wasn't how the battle was supposed to go. Innocent humans were suffering, and it was their fault. The Dragon of Death was much stronger than they had anticipated. Were they wrong to try to stop her? Would more suffer because of the battle they'd decided to fight with her? For the first time, he saw the awful pain that the Dragon of Death could inflict on others. He could picture clearly the type of world that the Dragon of Death would rule and realized with dread that he had seen it before – in the dream he had shared with Spark.

'I will protect as many people as I can,' said Buttons. 'For their sakes, and ours. She will be too powerful to stop if she takes all their life force.'

He turned to Dylan. 'I need your help,' he said, his voice shaking. 'Use our bond.'

Dylan nodded and closed his eyes. He took a deep breath and clenched his fists.

The protective bubble around them started to expand, pushing back the purple fog and bringing the residents of the palace into it. Once inside the bubble, they stopped writhing in pain, but lay motionless on the stone floor, the emperor among them.

'This is as far as I can push it!' said Buttons,

trembling with effort as the fog pounded against the walls of the bubble with the force of a thousand waves.

Charlotte stared at the bodies. 'Are they . . . dead?'

'They will live,' said Tank, 'but it will take time for them to recover.'

'Okay,' said Billy, relieved that they still had a chance. They hadn't lost yet. He pushed the vision of a world ruled by the Dragon of Death out of his mind. They had to save all these people. They couldn't let the Dragon of Death win.

'This is our one chance to stop the Dragon of Death for good,' said Spark. 'We must get the rest of the pearls away from them.'

'I don't know how long we can keep up the shield,' said Buttons through gritted teeth.

'We must act quickly,' said Tank.

'I want to take on Old Gold,' said Ling-Fei, her shoulders back. 'Xing and I are going to get the Flaming Pearl from him and the Dragon of Death.'

Xing nodded at Ling-Fei, proud.

'Charlotte and I will deal with these three new nox-wings,' thundered Tank.

'That leaves JJ and the Coral Pearl for me,' said

Billy. 'Spark, if you drop me off at the Great Wall, I'll take care of him. Da Huo is knocked out so he won't be an issue.'

'Good plan, Billy,' said Spark. 'I will leave you there to get the Coral Pearl and focus on the Dragon of Death. Xing will need my help.'

'Yes,' replied Xing. 'But we must all be careful to avoid the fog that she has created. If any part of it grips you, it will seep into you and take your life force to the Dragon of Death. If we fly fast enough out of the protective bubble, you will be safe. Just don't let it catch you. You have seen the agony it causes.'

'And be quick. I don't know how long I can hold off the fog,' said Buttons, his voice straining with effort.

'Let's go!' roared Tank, shooting out of the protective barrier towards the nox-wings.

Spark blasted out too and zoomed through the sky to the Great Wall. The fog was ice-cold. Billy briefly felt as if he were being hollowed out from the inside, the fog taking hold of him. Spark must have sensed Billy's fear because she gave a sudden surge forward. They punched through the noxious fog towards the

Great Wall where Da Huo lay unmoving, though still breathing.

'Find JJ and get the pearl,' said Spark as she landed on the Great Wall, next to the dragon-sized gap that Da Huo's body had left. 'Don't let the fog get you. I don't think you need to worry about Da Huo, but if he wakes, or if the fog comes, I will return.'

Billy slid off Spark, and she lowered her head, bringing it closer to Billy. *Be careful. JJ is stronger with his power. I know you want him to be a friend, but he is no longer on our side.* She gave Billy a reassuring nod and shot back towards the palace and the Dragon of Death.

Billy looked around. JJ had betrayed them, but that didn't mean he couldn't come back. Despite what Spark had said, Billy refused to believe he was evil. 'JJ, I know you're here somewhere. You don't have to stay with the Dragon of Death. You can still make the right choice and fight against the Noxious. I know you think the Dragon of Death will give you power, but dark magic will turn you rotten. And Spark has seen what will happen if she rules. It is not a world you want to be in.'

JJ leaped up from the other side of the wall, brushing dirt off his hands. He must have landed in the bushes beside the wall when Da Huo crashed. 'I don't need your pathetic advice. Stop trying to boss me around. Now give me your pearl. Or should I take it from you?' Without waiting for Billy to respond, JJ ran at him with incredible speed. Billy knew then he had made his choice and there was no turning back.

Just as JJ reached him, arm outstretched to grab Billy's pearl, Billy jumped into the air and somersaulted over him.

JJ slid to a stop and ran back towards Billy, his fists raised. 'Impressive. Let's see how much you picked up in your kung fu classes back at camp.' JJ threw a hundred punches and kicks at Billy in a matter of seconds. He spun and slashed through the air, each strike expertly delivered.

But Billy was faster. He didn't know much kung fu, but his agility allowed him to avoid JJ's attacks. And then he struck. He leaped into the air again and barrelled into JJ, knocking him over. JJ tried to fight back, but Billy was too quick. He snatched the pearl from JJ's neck and sprang back, clutching the Coral Pearl.

'JJ, please. I don't want to be your enemy.'

'You never learn, do you, Billy?' said JJ. He raised his voice. 'Da Huo!'

Billy saw the huge orange dragon shake his head and open his eyes. Fire shot out of his nostrils. Fear filled Billy. He was fast enough to beat JJ, but he could never take on a dragon by himself.

SPARK! JJ's dragon is awake!

With a *whoosh* of wings and a blast of crackling energy, Spark was there. And then JJ and Da Huo were frozen, trapped in an electric net. JJ's smug grin was fixed in place, but his eyes were still free to move. Billy saw that he was terrified. He felt a sharp twinge of something like regret for his almost friend. It shouldn't have come to this.

'Well done for getting the Coral Pearl,' said Spark. 'I am proud of you.' She thrummed with electricity, sparks flashing off her wings and antlers. Instead of being relieved by her heightened abilities, Billy felt alarmed. He wondered what had happened while they'd been apart to give her so much unexpected strength.

'You got back to me just in time,' said Billy. He didn't like to think what might have happened if Da Huo had attacked. 'How did you freeze them like that? Are they in pain?'

'I'm stronger now,' she said simply, ignoring his last question.

Billy wondered if he was imagining it when Spark's eyes flickered black for a moment. A tendril of dread slithered through him. He knew she must have been using dark magic, but there was no time to question it. They had to keep fighting.

She turned her gaze to Billy. 'Quick, we must help Xing and Ling-Fei fight the Dragon of Death and Old Gold.'

It felt wrong, leaving JJ terrified and frozen, huddled against his dragon, but there was nothing more Billy could do. They needed to stop the Dragon of Death, and if JJ was on her side then they needed to stop JJ too. But still Billy felt a pang of loss.

Billy and Spark flew back towards the palace, where Buttons was still protecting its residents from the noxious fog. Dylan was on Buttons's back, helping him keep the bubble intact through their bond. Even from a distance, Billy could see they were both exhausted. Sweat trickled down Dylan's face, and Buttons grimaced as he focused. Billy didn't know how much longer they could hold off the Noxious.

Xing and Ling-Fei were dodging attacks from the Dragon of Death, who was blasting purple fireballs in every direction. Billy saw Old Gold, still on his cloud, though now it looked as if he had lost control of it, and it swooped and dived like a loose balloon in a thunderstorm.

Billy realized that Ling-Fei was creating a whirlwind around herself and Xing to protect them from the fog. Hundreds of smoke tendrils shot towards them like torpedoes, before bursting into nothingness as they got close to the whirlwind. Ling-Fei's power must have been stronger too.

High above the palace, Tank and Charlotte were battling three nox-wings. Tank was bleeding from the wound Da Huo had inflicted earlier. He was keeping the two steel-grey dragons at bay with bared teeth and huge swipes from his claws when there was a flash of dark blue in the corner of Billy's vision. The midnight blue nox-wing was diving in from behind.

Charlotte spotted the blue nox-wing first, and, to Billy's amazement, she leaped off Tank's head, her fist pulled back, and delivered a powerful punch right on the dragon's nose. Its head whipped backwards. Tank turned and swiftly clamped down on the dragon's throat, twisting its neck as he did. Its body went limp and Tank let it fall, crashing into one of the palace's towers below. Clouds of purple fog shot upwards.

Charlotte was also falling through the sky, but, as Tank dived to get her, one of the steel-grey dragons wrapped its tail round his neck, and the other started blasting him with fireballs.

Billy felt a rush of panic from Spark through their bond. *We must be quick, Billy. You get Charlotte, and I will save Tank.*

But Billy was already running and jumping off Spark as she spat out a ball of ice that formed into a surfboard. He landed seamlessly on the moving ice and sped towards Charlotte. Spark was controlling the ice beneath his feet, but, through their bond,

Billy could move the board exactly as he wanted to. It was as if Billy were surfing the sky.

He swooped down and caught Charlotte in his arms.

'Nice punch,' Billy said, grinning.

Charlotte smiled back. 'Nice catch.'

Billy was relieved that she was okay. 'Let's go back and—'

'Watch out!' screamed Charlotte.

Billy felt a jolt run through his body as he spotted a huge cloud of purple fog drifting up from the palace towards him and Charlotte. It was already close. He pushed forward, going as fast as he could, but the fog was faster. It licked at the end of his surfboard.

'Shoo!' said Charlotte, waving her arms at the cloud, but it was no use.

Panic coursed through Billy as the fog crept up the board. He forced himself to take a breath and tried to prepare himself mentally for the pain of having his life force drained.

And then something miraculous happened.

As he watched the end of his board, he saw his foot disappear into thin air. He looked back at Charlotte, and, while he could still feel her weight in his arms, he couldn't see her.

Billy darted the board left, turning back towards the palace, and felt a huge sense of relief when the fog kept going forward, moving further and further away from them.

He looked at the palace and saw that Dylan was still gripping Buttons with one hand, but he held his other hand, trembling with effort, out towards Billy and Charlotte. Dylan had used his powers to hide them from the fog.

Now that they had escaped, Dylan let his hand drop, visibly relieved, and Billy and Charlotte flickered back into sight.

Billy grinned at his friend across the sky, thanking him.

'That was close,' said Charlotte. 'Now get us back to Tank!'

Above them, Spark had freed Tank from the grip of the steel-grey dragon, but Tank was badly injured, and Spark was now doing all the fighting.

Billy raced towards them. He could sense through his bond that Spark was feeling desperate.

I'm coming, Billy told her.

Stay back, she responded, to Billy's surprise. *You must trust me, Billy.*

Before he understood what she was doing, Spark spun in a tight circle, her whole body sizzling with electricity, and a ball of lightning forming in her mouth. Even from a distance, Billy felt her thrumming with energy. Her eyes flickered from gold to black. The two steel-grey dragons flapped back in surprise.

Spark stopped spinning, a dense tangle of electricity in her mouth. She spat an electric ball at one of the dragons. It struck the nox-wing and burst into a web of lightning bolts, ensnaring the creature like a net. Before the other dragon could react, Spark had shot a second ball of electricity and captured it as well.

Billy flew over to Tank and Spark.

'Tank, are you okay?' Charlotte asked. She jumped onto his back, rubbing her hands gently on his scales.

'I will be fine,' said Tank, but his voice sounded weak.

'Go back inside the protective bubble,' said Spark. 'Buttons will heal you. I'll take care of these two.'

Tank nodded and flew with Charlotte back to the palace.

Billy didn't have time to say anything else to Spark before he felt a chill run through his blood. The two nox-wings Spark had captured started to shake uncontrollably. He knew in his heart and he could feel through their bond that she was using dark magic to drain their life force. 'Spark!' he cried.

She ignored him. The nox-wings flailed until the life left their eyes and they lay limp in the air, still trapped in Spark's net. With a flip of her wings, the nets disappeared, and the dragons hurtled to the ground.

Billy swallowed hard. Seeing Spark kill another dragon, even a nox-wing, felt awful.

'One dragon left,' said Spark. She conjured another ball of electricity in her mouth. And this time she was aiming at the Dragon of Death.

Billy watched as the electric ball flashed through the sky, faster than a shooting star, heading directly for the Dragon of Death, who was still battling Xing and controlling the noxious fog.

The ball struck the Dragon of Death, and Billy felt the air quiver as her head snapped back and then her whole body stiffened as her limbs shot outwards as if she were being electrocuted.

'Great One!' yelled Old Gold, but, as he moved towards her, Xing blocked him, and Ling-Fei reached out and snatched the Flaming Pearl from around his neck. Immediately Old Gold's cloud disappeared, and he began to fall.

Xing caught him with her tail, dangling him upside down by his foot. 'You deserve to die. You are lucky my Ling-Fei has a good heart and would not wish that even on you,' she said. 'But you are evil to the core, like the dragon you serve. And you will share her fate.'

The Dragon of Death was writhing in the sky now, still fighting furiously against the electric bolts. Billy sensed the power emanating from her. With a great burst, she broke free.

'How dare you!' she roared. She flew directly at Spark, noxious fumes billowing from her mouth.

Spark sent another blast of crackling energy, more powerful than the last, directly at the Dragon of Death's heart.

As it hit her, the Dragon of Death screamed and froze in mid-air. Trapped in Spark's energy net.

Caught at last.

26

A Tainted Victory

They had done it. They had defeated the Dragon of Death.

'Quick!' shouted Xing. 'We must bring her back to the Dragon Realm. We do not want to cause any more destruction in this realm. And to banish her will require a powerful and dangerous enchantment.'

With tremendous exertion and focus, Spark combined the energy nets holding Da Huo and JJ with the larger one holding the Dragon of Death, and then drew the ball of electric energy towards her. Billy could feel Spark's power thrumming through her body and down their bond. It was unfamiliar and Billy didn't like it. He knew it was dark magic. But he also knew she was doing what had to be done.

When Spark's ball of electric energy was close enough, Xing dropped Old Gold inside. He froze instantly, mouth open in anger. JJ floated next to him, eyes still wide. Billy hated seeing him trapped like that. And he didn't know what would happen to JJ now. Would he face the same fate as the Dragon of Death and Old Gold?

All around them humans were gasping for breath as the energy that the Dragon of Death had been sucking from them flowed back.

The emperor stood and staggered towards where Xing and Ling-Fei were standing at the base of the Imperial Palace.

'I'm so sorry,' said Ling-Fei in Chinese. 'We did not mean for this to happen.'

To Billy's shock, Xing spoke to the emperor too, dipping her head respectfully. 'We cannot fix your palace or raise your dead. Or give you back the Diamond Pearl, but I will leave you with this.' Carefully she bit off one of her scales and tossed it to him. 'As proof of what you saw today. Remember – not all dragons are evil.'

The emperor fell to his knees as he accepted the scale.

'We must hurry,' said Tank. 'Spark will not be able to hold Da Huo and the Dragon of Death for long.' He took a deep breath. 'I do not have it in me to kill Da Huo. He was once our friend. Instead, he will be banished along with the Dragon of Death. I would destroy her if I could, but she cannot be killed. Only banished as far as we can send her.'

Billy stared at their frozen faces, caught in the ball of electric power. Before he looked away, he could have sworn the Dragon of Death grinned. It was a grin that chilled him to the bone. He shook his head – it must have been his imagination, surely. Why would she be smiling? They'd caught her. Finally. They had won. There was nothing she could do to them now.

'Billy,' said Xing, flying up to him. 'How is Spark? Will she be able to keep them trapped as we travel back?'

Spark was so focused on containing Da Huo

and the Dragon of Death, as well as JJ and Old Gold, she couldn't speak, even to respond to the other dragons.

Billy reached out through their bond.

And what he felt shocked him to his core.

Spark was drawing power from the Dragon of Death. In the exact way that the Dragon of Death had taken power from others. Billy felt dizzy with the realization. The lines between good and evil and justice and revenge had blurred beyond recognition. It felt wrong, but it was *Spark*. His dragon. He knew her heart. He wanted to think that she was just doing what she had to do, for the good of them all.

Billy tried to communicate with her, but she was so focused on what she was doing, it felt as if their bond were a fraying thread.

But he could also tell that she was stronger than she'd ever been and that she'd have no trouble bringing the Noxious dragons back to their realm.

He knew he couldn't tell the others about what Spark was doing. They wouldn't understand. She was doing it for the greater good, he tried to tell himself. But deep down Billy knew there was a difference between defence and what Spark was doing. He didn't want to admit it to himself, but he couldn't deny what was happening. Spark was using the very dark magic they were all fighting against.

But then... If this was the price to stop the Dragon of Death for good, it was worth it, wasn't it? Spark would explain everything to everyone when they were back. That was the important thing. Getting back to the Dragon Realm.

'She can make it,' he said. 'But Tank's right, we should go now.'

'Is everything okay?' said Ling-Fei, concerned. 'You're very pale.'

'I'm fine,' said Billy curtly. 'Let's just get out of here.'

They left the ruined palace and flew back to the lake.

Spark flew in the middle, the two dragons trapped in her electric net trailing behind her. Buttons flew at the rear, Tank in the front, and Xing soared above them, keeping a close eye on the trapped dragons.

They dived into the lake, and Xing cast the same protective enchantment as before so the humans could breathe. In the dark, watery depths, the

Dragon of Death's glowing red eyes shone fiercely, and Billy felt as if they were following him.

Spark, are you okay? he thought.

But there was no response other than the surge of power humming through her.

It will all be over soon, Billy told himself. *We'll imprison the Dragon of Death. Spark will be back to normal. We'll go home. The Human and Dragon Realms will be safe again. It will all be worth it.*

They emerged into the Dragon Realm and landed on the shores of the lake. It was midday here, the oval sun high in the sky next to the ever-present triple moons. They were still in the past.

As soon as Spark touched her feet to the ground, Billy leaped off, eager to be away from the strange magic thrumming through her. It was the first time since he'd bonded with Spark that he had wanted to be apart from her. Somewhere in his mind, the fear that Spark's dabbling in dark magic would taint him began to grow, but he pushed it down. Spark was good. He knew it. She was his dragon. She had to be.

The Dragon of Death, Da Huo, Old Gold and JJ were all still frozen in place.

'So . . . what happens now?' said Dylan nervously.

'JJ and Old Gold will both have to be incapacitated, of course,' said Tank. 'But there are ways that do not involve more killing. The old man will present a challenge, though once we have dealt with the Dragon of Death, and our old friend Da Huo, he won't be nearly as much of a problem. People on their own against dragons rarely are.'

'That's the bit I don't understand. How are you going to deal with an all-powerful evil dragon once we unfreeze her?' said Dylan.

'As you know, she cannot be killed. And so she will be sent into the sky and turned into a star,' said Buttons.

'Well, that doesn't sound so bad,' said Charlotte.

'She will be so far and so distant that her light will not shine on either realm. Until she is swallowed by a black hole, and then it will not shine at all,' added Xing.

'That sounds a bit more intense,' said Billy. 'Why a star?'

'All dragons turn into stars eventually and live on

through their light,' said Xing. Then she turned to Ling-Fei. 'Your name for me is especially fitting.'

'Even for the Dragon of Death, it is a kind end. Kinder than she deserves. The same goes for Da Huo,' said Tank.

Billy didn't think his heart could beat harder than it was, but hearing that made it race even faster. 'So ... when Spark swallowed a star ...'

If Spark heard, she gave no indication of it. She kept her unwavering focus on their trapped enemies.

'Not every star is a dragon,' said Buttons gently. 'Though there is a chance. She would have known the risk.'

'Dabbling in dark magic does not come without a cost,' said Xing.

So the dragons had known that Spark was using dark magic when she had swallowed that star.

'But ...' said Billy. He wanted to tell them that swallowing the star had changed Spark, and he was worried she might be turning Noxious. But he didn't want to betray his dragon.

'Enough questions,' said Tank. 'We are wasting time. Children, trust us. And step back.'

The four of them did as they were told. Billy felt a small tickle on his shoulder and looked over.

It was the small flying gold pig. Despite everything, he smiled. He felt as if he were meeting an old friend. 'Nice to see you again,' he said to it.

'Unfreeze them, Spark. But keep them restrained,' said Tank.

'This seems like a bad idea,' muttered Dylan. 'Can't we just catapult them into the sky like that in their neat frozen bubble?'

'We can't send JJ and Old Gold up into space,' said Ling-Fei.

'I still don't know what we're going to do with them,' said Charlotte darkly.

Billy heard his friends talking quietly, but he barely registered what they were saying. All he could focus on was Spark. Even though he was no longer physically next to her, he could still feel that strange power revving through her. It felt *wrong*.

Spark reared her head back and shook it, once to the left, once to the right. The ball of electricity around her captors split, and JJ and Old Gold went one way, and Da Huo and the Dragon of Death another.

JJ and Old Gold collapsed in a heap next to each other. JJ slowly raised his head, and Billy saw his eyes were bloodshot. Old Gold didn't move at all.

'What ... did ... you ... do ... to ... us?' JJ choked out between gasping breaths.

'I didn't think you'd harm the humans,' Buttons said mildly to Spark. 'That's not like you.'

'It was necessary,' said Spark in a tone Billy barely recognized. 'I needed to make sure they were subdued.'

Da Huo lay unresponsive on the ground as bolts of electricity wrapped round him, keeping him trapped.

The Dragon of Death stood before them. Silent but watchful. Bolts of electricity shimmered around her, pinning her wings together, clamping her jaws shut and chaining her feet to the ground.

'Together,' said Tank. He looked the Dragon of Death in the eye. 'Old foe, we send you now and for ever far away, where you may never do harm again.'

'We need the pearls first,' Spark interrupted, in her unfamiliar tone. 'Give them to me – quickly.'

Charlotte put her hand on her Gold Pearl. 'But ... it's my pearl.'

'The dragons need them,' said Billy. He wanted to defend Spark – he still hoped that she knew what she was doing. He couldn't let himself lose faith in her. Not now.

'My pearl belonged to my grandmother,' said Ling-Fei softly. 'It doesn't feel right to hand it over.'

'The pearls!' said Spark. 'We have no time to lose! Give them to me!'

'Come on,' said Charlotte. 'This is it. We knew it would come to this. We have to use the pearls to defeat the Dragon of Death once and for all.' She took hers off and handed it to Spark. Dylan and Ling-Fei did the same.

Billy waited a moment. He had his Lightning Pearl, as well as the Flaming Pearl and the Coral Pearl that he had taken from Old Gold and JJ.

'Give them to me, Billy,' said Spark.

He handed them all to her. 'Here,' he said, looking up at Spark. 'Now we can finally end this.' This was the right thing to do, it had to be.

Spark took the pearls in her claws. 'Thank you, Billy,' she said. She looked him in the eye. 'I hope you can forgive me.'

Then she turned back to the Dragon of Death.

But not before Billy saw her eyes fade to black.

'NO!' he said, lunging forward.

It was too late.

Spark released the Dragon of Death and handed over all eight pearls.

The Destiny Bringer

Everything happened very fast after that.

Tank, Buttons and Xing roared, but Spark threw a ball of electricity to freeze them in place the way she had the Dragon of Death.

'I'm sorry, my friends,' she said. She turned to the Dragon of Death and dipped her head. 'I see now that your power is limitless and joining you is the only way. Even while I was drawing on your life force, I could only contain you for so long. I've never encountered power like it. And I crave more of it.'

The Dragon of Death unfurled her wings and stretched her long, sinuous neck. She said nothing, but grinned at the eight pearls now in her grasp.

'What is happening?' Dylan said. 'Billy! Do something! Stop her!'

'I can't,' said Billy, his voice choked with emotion. Anger, sadness, fear and guilt warred within him. 'Stay close.' They joined hands, and Billy waited for that special rush to go through him, the one that came from the four of them being together.

But there was nothing. The power of their togetherness wasn't enough against the Dragon of Death. Not without their pearls and their dragons.

JJ lay next to an unconscious Old Gold, watching. Billy figured he wouldn't be afraid. After all, JJ had joined the Dragon of Death's side, and he knew what she was capable of. But he looked wary.

'You traitor!' Charlotte spat at Spark.

'Why?' said Ling-Fei, sounding pained. 'Spark, this is not you.'

'I thought you were going to fight it,' Billy said. 'Fight the Noxious. You said you would.' He was holding back tears. He'd never believed it would come to this. How could Spark betray them? How could she betray *him*? Worst of all, he had helped her by keeping quiet and convincing her not to tell the others. If they had known, maybe they could have stopped it from happening.

'You knew?' Dylan said, aghast. Billy hung his head. He couldn't look at his friends. He couldn't face the betrayal they must all be feeling.

The Dragon of Death looked up. 'How charming,' she purred. 'The humans are sad. Little mortals, dry your tears. Save your strength. A new reign is coming. You will know your place.' She looked appraisingly at Spark. 'And how truly divine that you were the one to bring me what I need. You know I knew your mother?'

Spark seemed to shrink beneath the Dragon of Death's gaze. 'My mother?' she said, sounding dazed.

'She was one of my great warriors. The most powerful dragon I'd ever encountered, second only to myself. We were unstoppable. But then she wanted to have a hatchling. And suddenly my most trusted fighter cared about goodness more than power. She disappeared in the night, hiding in a cave to lay her egg.' The Dragon of Death licked her sharp teeth. 'Of course, I took my revenge. Loyalty is my most valued virtue. I would have destroyed you too, but you disappeared. I am so pleased that you escaped, now that you are the one who has delivered everything I've ever wanted.' She cackled, and the sound made Billy's bones hurt. 'Your blood was noxious already. Just waiting to come out. Tell me, young Spark, when you had your first taste of dark magic, did it taste like home?'

Spark seemed to come back to herself, the Spark that Billy knew, and she let out an agonized cry. 'I swallowed my first star to protect my human. I thought I would be strong enough to resist the pull of dark magic.' Billy flinched. Her words physically hurt him. 'I destroyed my hoard for the portal, but I did it knowing the rush of power it would bring.' Billy looked at the other three dragons, trapped, but able to hear and see everything. Tank's jaws were unhinged, his mouth wide open, ready to unleash fire that would now never come. Xing was coiled like a spring, about to strike. And Buttons's face was frozen in shock. Only their eyes moved, darting back and forth between Spark and the Dragon of Death. 'I thought I would be strong enough to manage it. I thought that this was the only way we would be able to defeat you once and for all,' Spark went on.

'Then what happened, little seer?'

'I took life force during the battle. And, when I trapped you and Da Huo, I began to draw on your life force too. It was the only way I thought I would be strong enough to keep you contained. But it was too much. The power running through me overpowered my fight to resist the Noxious. And I could tell that even with me taking your life force, you were still so strong. The power you have is irresistible. I would do anything to keep that power for myself.'

'It's all been for nothing,' Billy cried out. 'We believed in you! How could you, Spark?' He was crying now. 'You said yourself you saw the devastation she will bring. How could you let it happen?' She'd told him she was struggling to fight the darkness, but he thought she would win. She should have been stronger. He should have done more to help her. To save her from herself.

'I'm sorry, Billy. I couldn't stop myself.'

She looked at the Dragon of Death. 'Please do not

283

hurt the human children or my former friends. For me, do this.'

The Dragon of Death sniffed. 'How disgustingly sentimental of you. I'll allow it on one condition. They will take their place in my new world.'

Billy knew with terrifying certainty that Spark's visions – the visions they'd been working so hard to stop – were about to come true. The death and destruction and despair. It was all going to happen. They'd failed. He'd failed. And now the whole world was going to suffer. His friends. His family. Everyone. The Dragon of Death dropped the eight pearls on the ground and arranged them in a sideways figure of eight.

The symbol for infinity.

The pearls began to glow increasingly brighter until it hurt to look at them and they were connected by a stream of bright pulsing light. The stream went faster and faster and faster, like a race car zooming round a track. Suddenly, the pearls disappeared.

And then the oval sun fell out of the sky.

The sun landed with a wet thump and cracked open. Yellow light spilled out.

The sun was smaller than Billy would have imagined

a sun to be, about a metre and a half wide. He stepped away from the yellow light that spilled out like yolk from an egg.

It was the only light in the world. Everywhere else was dark.

Billy wanted to go to Spark. He wanted her wings to light up with electricity. He wanted her to comfort him.

But she was their enemy now. She sat behind the Dragon of Death. Billy sensed her staring at him, but he wouldn't look at her. He couldn't.

He felt her trying to talk to him through their bond, but the wall he had put up in his mind was impenetrable. Just as she had blocked him out, now he refused to let her in. She sounded like a faraway whisper, words he couldn't make out. Words he didn't want to make out.

'Billy, I'm sorry!' Spark cried out loud.

The Dragon of Death hissed and shot a thread of electricity at Spark, muzzling her.

'Silence! Your attachment to your human bores me.'

Spark whimpered, just once, and the sound cut into Billy's soul.

Still he kept the wall between them.

She had betrayed them all. She had betrayed their bond. And he would never forgive her.

The Dragon of Death seemed to be waiting for something. She stared at the cracked sun with fierce concentration.

The sun quivered. And then the top popped off, as if something were trying to get out of it. And a head poked out of the sun.

At first, Billy thought it was a small dragon, but as the creature wriggled its way out, taking the bright light with it, he realized it was a turtle.

It stared at them all with large round eyes. 'Who has summoned me?' it croaked in a wizened voice.

'Destiny Bringer,' said the Dragon of Death respectfully, dropping her neck in a bow. 'It is I. I placed the Eight Great Treasures together in the symbol.'

'So you have,' said the Destiny Bringer.

'Is that a . . . turtle?' whispered Dylan.

'Why are there humans here?' said the Destiny Bringer. 'And such young ones!' Its already wrinkled face wrinkled more in confusion. 'Are you sure the humans did not summon me?'

'It was I!' roared the Dragon of Death.

'Remember your place, dragon,' ordered the Destiny Bringer. 'I am bound by the summons, but do not test my patience. I decide the details of the destiny.'

The turtle stood on its short hind legs – it was shorter than Billy – and hobbled over to where the pearls had been. 'Now, how does it go again? It has been a long time since I've been summoned. Oh, yes.' It lowered its voice and said, *'Many futures await; one destiny of eight. When much is at stake, it is your choice to make.'*

'Show me,' said the Dragon of Death. 'Show me my destinies.'

The turtle clapped its front feet and eight images appeared where the pearls had been. Billy recognized one immediately. It was the one he'd seen in his nightmare. The one that Spark had seen in her visions.

A tall skyscraper with a dragon wrapped round it. And not just any dragon.

The Dragon of Death.

Another one showed her flying with an army of dragons over an ocean. And another had her sleeping, curled up in front of a huge hoard of gold treasure. Another showed her on top of a volcano.

They were all single images, but Billy could tell that the Dragon of Death saw more in them than he did.

She turned to look at him and his friends.

'I know you think I am evil. The most evil creature in all the realms, in all the times. And perhaps I am. But know this too. I could choose a destiny with no humans ever again. But I do not want that. So consider me merciful. You four, as well as my faithful servants, JJ and Jin, will be the only humans to remember what came before the new time. Tell all how merciful I am. Worship me the way I deserve, and you may live.' She looked back at the Destiny Bringer turtle. 'I have chosen my destiny.'

With a flick of her wing, she indicated the one that Billy had known she was going to choose. The one with skyscrapers and darkness and flames. The destiny he and his friends had been doing everything to try to prevent.

The Destiny Bringer turtle nodded. 'Your chosen destiny awaits.'

Light billowed round the turtle, and, as it spread, it

wiped away the very fabric of existence. The Dragon of Death began to laugh, even as she disappeared in the light.

'Don't let go of each other,' Billy whispered fiercely to his friends. 'We'll find you!' he yelled out to their dragons. 'Don't forget us! Don't give up!'

Before the light overtook him, the Destiny Bringer looked at Billy and winked.

And then everything disappeared.

A Dark Future

Billy opened his eyes.

The first thing he noticed was the noise. Clanking, clanging, buzzing sounds and loud shouting reverberated through his ears.

The second thing he noticed were the people. There were people *everywhere*. Marching in lines, getting on trucks and drilling into the earth, using huge machines he'd never seen before.

The third thing he noticed were the shackles and chains around his wrists and ankles.

Next to him were Dylan, Charlotte and Ling-Fei. Their eyes were closed, and their faces were bruised and dirty, but they seemed to be breathing. Ling-Fei was resting her head on Charlotte's shoulder. Dylan still had his glasses on.

They weren't in their protective suits any longer.

They were dressed in ragged grey clothes. The same clothes all the other people in this place were wearing.

Gradually Billy realized they were sitting on the side of what looked like an incredibly busy road, and they were chained to a building. He tilted his head back. Black and purple buildings towered above. They all hummed and buzzed with electricity. He looked up at the sky. It was grey and smoggy, but he could still see the sun. It was a round sun, the sun of the Human Realm.

Where are we? Billy thought. *And where are our dragons? And JJ and Old Gold?* He knew he should be terrified – they were in the Dragon of Death's chosen future – but instead he felt numb with shock and exhaustion.

Just then there was a flittering next to his ear, and a squeak.

It was the small flying pig! How had it come here with them into this destiny?

'Hey there,' said Billy. 'Wasn't expecting to see you again.' But he was so glad to see the small pig; it felt like meeting an old friend. It gave him a boost of much-needed energy.

The pig squeaked, as if trying to get his attention. Then Billy heard a loud bellow. A familiar bellow. He frantically looked around, trying to see where the sound was coming from.

Yes! There was Tank! His mighty wings were pinned back so he couldn't fly. He was being prodded with sharp glowing sticks by other dragons. Noxious dragons.

'Stop causing trouble!' shouted one of the nox-wings. 'I don't even know what a big dragon like you is doing above ground. You should be in the tunnels. You've got digging to do.'

A silver blur whooshed by. Xing! She was here too! Billy could have sworn she smiled down at them.

'Someone catch that dragon!' the nox-wing who had been shouting at Tank yelled. 'Or we'll all face the wrath of the Great One!'

And then, closer now, a familiar song.

Buttons was nearby, and he was singing his

healing song. Billy felt the aches in his body start to melt away.

'Stop that singing! Get back to work!' shouted another Noxious dragon.

The song was abruptly cut off, but it had done its job. Billy no longer felt exhausted – he felt rejuvenated. And hopeful. Their dragons were here! They weren't alone. He felt a pang as he remembered that *his* dragon, Spark, was no longer on their side, but at least Tank, Buttons and Xing were all here in this future. And so were his friends.

'Guys, wake up!' he whispered as loudly as he dared. Dylan's eyes flew open and widened as he took in everything around them. Ling-Fei's eyes opened slowly, and she took a few deep breaths. Charlotte blinked and strained against her shackles. Nothing. 'Worth a try,' she said with a shrug. 'Where are we? Or *when* are we?'

'There is so much pain and suffering,' said Ling-Fei, shivering slightly. 'I can feel it even without my pearl.'

'We're in some sort of city. In the future, I think,' said Billy. 'The future the Dragon of Death wanted.'

He took a deep breath and looked at his friends. 'And we aren't in the Dragon Realm any more. We're back in our world. Our world has been taken over by the Noxious and the Dragon of Death.'

'This is the worst possible outcome,' said Dylan. 'I think I'm in shock. I'm not even scared.'

'Deep breaths,' said Ling-Fei gently. Then she started to cough. 'Never mind. The air here is terrible. What have they done to the world?'

'Billy, I recognize that look in your eye. What are you thinking?' said Charlotte.

'Dylan's wrong. This isn't the worst possible outcome. We're together, aren't we? And our dragons are here too.' He paused and cleared his throat. 'I mean, your dragons are here. I don't have a dragon any more.' The pain of Spark's betrayal gripped his heart.

'But you've got us,' said Ling-Fei.

'And the pig is back too!' said Dylan.

'Our powers might be gone, but we didn't need them to open the mountain,' said Charlotte. 'Billy is right. We've got each other, and that is what has always made us strong.'

The four friends looked at one another and smiled. Billy felt a small flicker of hope light up inside him. 'The Dragon of Death hasn't won yet,' he said. 'We're still here. And we're still fighting. It's up to us to change this destiny. To change everything. To save everyone.'

'I'm impressed with your optimism, as always, but how exactly are we going to do that if we are chained up? We need someone to save us before we can save the world,' said Dylan.

'We can't give up now,' said Charlotte. 'This is just a minor setback.'

'That's one way of putting it,' muttered Dylan.

Billy leaned towards his friends, his grin growing. 'Don't worry. I've got a plan.' He lowered his voice and told the others what he was thinking.

'That will never work,' said Dylan, shaking his head.

'It has to work,' said Charlotte. 'We don't have any other options.'

'I believe in us,' said Ling-Fei, eyes shining. 'We can do it.'

'I guess it is better than nothing,' said Dylan. 'Fine, fine. I'm in.'

'That's the spirit,' said Billy.

The plan wasn't perfect, but it was a start. The friends drew closer together, and Billy felt a familiar jolt of energy run through them – the energy that came from when they worked together – and he was suddenly filled with hope. Ling-Fei was right. Together, they could do this. They *would* do this.

After all, they were humanity and dragonkind's only hope.

ACKNOWLEDGEMENTS

When we started writing *Dragon Mountain*, we had no idea that it would be the start of such an exciting adventure for us as authors. The publication experience has been such a dream – and we have loved seeing so many readers discover our dragons. And we are even more excited that the adventure continues in *Dragon Legend*.

We have a dragon-size list of people to thank for helping us get our dragons out into the world!

To our amazing agent, Claire Wilson, for being the best agent in all the land, including the human and dragon realms. Much like the Destiny Bringer, she has made our dream life/future come true!

Thank you as well to the rest of the team at RCW, especially Safae El-Ouahabi for her support and to Sam Coates for taking our dragons global.

To Rachel Denwood at Simon & Schuster, for her unwavering belief in our dragons and her vision for them and for us. It is a tremendous privilege to work with you and be published by you. Long may you reign as our dragon queen!

To the wonderful Lucy Rogers who edited *Dragon Mountain* and *Dragon Legend* and made them the best books they could be – thank you for your brilliance and your kindness. We will miss working with you, but you will always be Team Dragon to us.

We'd also like to thank Ali Dougal, Jenny Glencross and Lowri Ribbons on the editorial team for all their support for the series. And welcome to Team Dragon, Amina Youssef! Thank you for getting *Dragon Legend* ready to fly and starting work on book three with us.

Thank you to Catherine Coe, who is the dream copyeditor – her suggestions are always spot on and she gets our jokes. A huge thank you as well to our proofreader, Jane Tait, for her excellent proofread and making the book shine.

Speaking of shine, we still can't get over how beautiful and shiny the covers for the books are! Thank you to Jesse Green in design, Tom Sanderson for the gorgeous lettering, and, of course, the phenomenally talented illustrator Petur Antonsson, who so perfectly brought our dragons to life. The *Dragon Legend* cover is just as beautiful, if not more so, than *Dragon Mountain*. We'd also like to thank Sophie Storr in production for her work on the book.

Dragon Mountain soared out into the world in supreme style thanks to the dream team in marketing, sales, and PR at Simon & Schuster. A huge thank you to the entire team, but especially Laura Hough and Danielle Wilson in sales, Sarah Macmillan and Sarah Garmston in marketing, and our fantastic publicist Eve Wersocki Morris. Launching a book during a global pandemic is a bit of a challenge, and our team did such an incredible job getting the book out there to as many readers as possible. We can't wait to see you all in real life when it is safe to do so to thank you and celebrate properly.

An audiobook brings a book to life in a very special way and we are so happy that readers can listen to *Dragon Legend* thanks to Dominic Brendon at Simon & Schuster and our amazing narrator, Kevin Shen. So many readers let us know how much they loved the first audiobook!

We are tremendously grateful to booksellers around the world for supporting us and our books. Special thank you to Queen's Park Books, Chicken & Frog, Tales on Moon Lane and Waterstones. We'd also like to especially thank Florentyna Martin; we are so glad you saw something special in *Dragon Mountain*.

We also want to thank all the teachers and librarians who have championed the series! Special thanks to Karen Wall and Scott Evans.

We are very lucky to have the support of so many author friends, who we adore and admire. Thank you to Kiran Millwood Hargrave, Roshani Chokshi, Samantha Shannon, Catherine Doyle, Abi Elphinstone, Katherine Woodfine, Anna James and Katherine Rundell for their generous and wonderful quotes and support for the series. You are all amazing humans, who we are very lucky to know!

Thank you to Kevin's childhood friend, Nathan Bell, for inspiring the last name 'Bell' for Charlotte. And thank you to Katie's oldest and dearest friends, Fay and Janou Gordon, for a childhood full of imagination and wonder. Speaking of the Dewberry crew, special hello and thanks to David Garcia, Max Scott, Veronica La Frossia, Lee Gordon and, of course, Diego.

We'd also like to thank Jessica and Allen Leech for their ongoing support and enthusiasm for our books – we can't wait for Poppy to one day read them.

We wrote the acknowledgements for the first *Dragon Mountain* book at the start of the 2020 Covid-19 pandemic, and never imagined that by the time we were writing the acknowledgements for the second book in late 2020, the pandemic would still be ongoing. What a year it has been. We want to thank all the healthcare and key workers for keeping us safe in this time, with a special thank you to our friend Dr Thomas Getreu (and shout-out to his two adorable kids, Carson and Cameran).

And finally, to our wonderful family across the globe. Thank you to the far-flung Tsang, Webber,

Hopper and Liu family members for their incredible support. It means so much that you all are still so excited every time we have a new book. We are especially appreciative to Katie's Aunt Nancy, Aunt Liz, Uncle Jon, Aunt Ceal and Uncle Dave for their enthusiasm and support! And, of course, a special thank you to our parents, Virginia and Rob Webber and Louisa and Paulus Tsang, for everything. For watching our daughter so we could write and do events, for buying multiple copies and telling everyone about it and for always being there.

We both have the best siblings, and in-laws, anyone could wish for. To Stephanie, Ben and Cooper in Georgia; to Jack and Cat in Ireland; and to Janie in California (and sometimes Seattle). We love you all so much.

And to our daughter, Evie, who has been with us from the very start of our Dragon adventure. You've made what could have otherwise been a very tough year a remarkable and joyful one. You'll always be our baby dragon.

KATIE & KEVIN TSANG met in 2008 while studying at the Chinese University of Hong Kong. Since then they have lived on three different continents and travelled to over 40 countries together. As well as the DRAGON REALM series, they are the co-writers of the young fiction series SAM WU IS NOT AFRAID (Egmont) and Katie also writes YA as Katherine Webber.

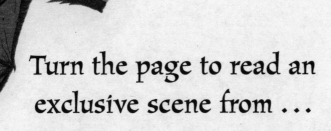

Turn the page to read an
exclusive scene from ...

DRAGON
CITY

Coming September 2021!

When the bells began to toll as the city's neon lights flickered on and the sky grew dark, Billy, Charlotte, Ling-Fei and Dylan kept to the shadows.

The streets were lined with huge buildings, each big enough to house dragons. They had gigantic windows and doors that dragons flew in and out of. And in the centre of the city, a towering skyscraper stretched high into the clouds. It radiated with pulsing electricity and purple smoke poured out of the windows.

'We should stay far from that tower,' said Ling-Fei, eyeing it with unease. 'It feels evil.'

The four friends hurried through the dark, careful to avoid any dragons, until they turned down a narrow alley and reached a sewer grate at the end. Billy paused. The feeling urging him onwards was stronger here, drawing him closer, like someone cold seeking heat.

He looked at his friends and swallowed. 'I think we should go underground.'

A voice from the dark slithered out. 'A good idea, boy, a good idea indeed.' And then a tall, thin figure emerged from the shadows. It was a woman in a black cloak with silver hair down to her waist. But her face was young and smooth. Most alarming of all was the glowing knife gripped in her hand and the net thrown over her shoulder. She caught Billy staring and flashed him a sharp grin.

'That's right, I'm a nox-hand. I could get a fine reward for turning in humans, especially *young* humans, caught out after dark.'

Charlotte stepped forward, her hands on her hips. 'I'd like to see you try. In case you can't count, there are four of us and one of you.'

'Charlotte,' hissed Dylan in a high-pitched whisper, 'she has a *knife*. And we don't have our pearls!'

Charlotte shrugged, keeping her gaze on the cloaked woman. 'I could still knock her flat on her butt.'

Billy moved closer to Charlotte. If she was going to fight this woman, she wasn't going to do it on her own. Without saying a word, Ling-Fei did the same, and, after a short moment, even Dylan stepped forward, muttering under his breath. This woman didn't know what they had faced. They had battled a giant scorpion, conquered nox-wings and even defeated the Wasteland Worm. They were not afraid of a stranger with a cloak and a knife.

At least not *that* afraid.

The woman took another look at them, and then laughed, long and loud. 'Perhaps I won't turn you in. It would be a shame for all that energy to be sucked up into the Tower. Now run along, little rodents, before another nox-hand finds you. Or worse, a nox-wing. They won't find you as amusing as I do.'

She turned on her heel and strode into the dark, holding her knife aloft. When she reached the end of the alley, a long, turquoise dragon flew round the corner. Billy watched as it went straight for the woman, but then as it registered her glowing knife, it stopped short, and gave her a curt nod. The woman nodded back and disappeared into the shadows. The nox-wing raised its large head and looked straight at Billy. Its tongue flicked out, like it was licking its lips.

Billy gulped.

'Come on!' he said to his friends. He didn't want to wait to see what would happen when the nox-wing reached them. He yanked open the sewer grate. 'We've got to get out of here!'

'We don't know what's down there!' cried Dylan.

'It can't be worse than what's heading right towards us,' said Charlotte. 'I'm going in.' And with that, she slid into the dark.

'Hurry!' said Billy to the others. The nox-wing was forcing its way through the narrow alley, its snapping jaws getting closer with every second. They were running out of time.